P9-BYS-690

THE HEART TRIUMPHANT

In a few short hours Cerissa would have everything she thought she wanted.

A wealthy young lord was anxiously awaiting their wedding. Cerissa would become a great lady. No one would ever again mention her low birth.

Yet her heart pounded for the gallant young guardian who had seen her safely to England. Penniless as he was, it was Sheldon that Cerissa really loved.

But now he was leaving her in the care of the foolish lord who would be her husband. He would soon depart to another country and remain a lifetime away.

Cerissa was suddenly aware that her charade had worked perfectly. She had deceived everyone. But could she fool her own heart?

BARBARA CARTLAND

Bantam Books by Barbara Cartland
Ask your bookseller for the books you have missed

Barbara Cartland
The Heart Triumphant

BANTAM BOOKS · TORONTO · NEW YORK · LONDON

THE HEART TRIUMPHANT
A Bantam Book / December 1976

All rights reserved.
Copyright © 1976 by Barbara Cartland.
This book may not be reproduced in whole or in part, by
mimeograph or any other means, without permission.
For information address: Bantam Books, Inc.

ISBN 0-553-10338-5

Published simultaneously in the United States and Canada

Bantam Books are published by Bantam Books, Inc. Its trade-
mark, consisting of the words "Bantam Books" and the por-
trayal of a bantam, is registered in the United States Patent
Office and in other countries. Marca Registrada. Bantam
Books, Inc., 666 Fifth Avenue, New York, New York 10019.

PRINTED IN THE UNITED STATES OF AMERICA

Author's Note

Bath in 1793 was the most fashionable Spa in England. Its magnificent buildings, still in existence today, were just being completed, and its hot springs, "wonderful and most excellent, agaynst very many sicknesses," were as popular as they had been in Roman times.

The proprietary Chapels as described in this book are authentic—their history begins in 1730 in the Mayflower Chapel in Curzon Street, London, where the incumbent Dr. Alexander Keith performed seven hundred marriages in a year at one guinea each, while the regular parish Church solemnised only forty.

Chapter One
1793

The wind rattled the shutters and blew beneath the doors of the Inn, so that in the private Sitting-Room the gentleman sitting in front of the fire shivered.

It was to be expected that there should be storms in the Channel during January, and any possibility of making the crossing to England was unlikely for at least another twenty-four hours.

Sheldon Harcourt knew that he was fortunate in having obtained comfortable accommodation and a private room at the Hôtel d'Angleterre in Calais.

Monsieur Dessin, the Proprietor, was besieged by visitors, the majority of whom were English, hurrying out of France and returning with all possible speed to their own country.

News of the execution of the French King, Louis XVI, had fallen upon the English like a thunder-bolt.

In London the news was received at first with stupefied disbelief, then with horror, and finally with a burst of rage.

In France, to the tourists who were beginning to think that the country was settling down under the Convention, it spelt danger of internment.

It was obvious, even to the most obtuse traveller, that England would declare war on France.

Yet Sheldon Harcourt was exceedingly reluctant

to accept the inevitable and in his own words "to scuttle back across the Channel."

He had, however, been advised by his French friends that there was no alternative.

The massacre the previous August of the aristocrats, Bishops, and Priests, and the atrocities of the *Septembriseurs,* had made Paris a place of terror.

Sometimes Sheldon Harcourt thought that he would never again be free of the cries of people he had known and liked being dragged from their homes to the rapidly emptying prisons to provide more victims for the mob.

And yet, however reluctant he was to leave the country in which he had spent the last five years, and which until now he had thought of as his home, he looked unmistakably English as he sat back in a winged arm-chair and felt the warmth of the flames on his face.

It would be difficult to think that any man could be more handsome or more elegantly attired.

Despite three days of exhausting travel on the muddy and ill-kept roads, he looked as if he were just about to enter an Assembly.

His clothes fitted him to perfection, but he wore them with a casual elegance which was essentially English.

As he looked into the fire his blue eyes were very serious, but usually they twinkled mockingly at life, and his cynical smile when it twisted his lips drew into prominence the deep lines between his nose and mouth.

His thoughts were disturbed by the opening of the door as *Monsieur* Dessin entered, carrying a tray on which reposed a bottle of wine and a glass.

"I trust you are comfortable, *Milor?*" he enquired.

To him all Englishmen were noble, just as to the English all foreigners were considered to be inferior and for the most part half-witted!

"I am comfortable," Sheldon Harcourt replied, "but I am hoping dinner will not be long delayed."

"It will not, *Milor*. My wife is at this moment preparing special dishes to your liking. At the same time, we crave your indulgence because the Hotel is full."

"To your advantage!" Sheldon Harcourt remarked.

Monsieur Dessin shrugged his shoulders expressively.

"The Dining-Room is crammed with travellers who talk a lot, complain incessantly, and drink little."

"They are also excessively noisy!" Sheldon Harcourt remarked.

Through the open door he could hear the raised voices, riotous laughter, and continuous cry of:

"*Garçon! Garçon!*"

Monsieur Dessin poured out a glass of wine and handed it on the tray to Sheldon Harcourt.

He took a small sip, rolled it round his tongue, and nodded his head.

"Excellent!"

"It is *du meilleur, Milor*. I would not offer you anything else."

"You are wise!" Sheldon Harcourt remarked.

There was a hint of warning in his voice.

Monsieur Dessin hesitated.

"*Milor*, I have a favour to ask."

There was a pause and Sheldon Harcourt raised his eye-brows.

"A favour?" he repeated.

"The Dining-Room is full, and anyway the place is *pas convenable*, you will understand, for a Lady of Quality."

He looked at the Englishman apprehensively before he said:

"Would you, *Milor*, be most gracious and invite a lady of great distinction to dine with you? There is nowhere else I can accommodate her, nowhere at all!"

"I engaged this room for my private use," Sheldon Harcourt replied.

"I know, *Milor*, but this lady is young and beautiful, and to put her in the Dining-Room might cause

3

her to endure much unpleasantness. Her bed-chamber, you will understand, *Milor,* is cold."

Monsieur Dessin was pleading with Sheldon Harcourt, who gave him a sharp glance before he said:

"Young and beautiful? Are you sure?"

"Mais certainement, Milor! I swear you will not be disappointed. *Madame est belle—très belle!"*

As if to accentuate his words, *Monsieur* Dessin kissed his fingers and threw them out in an age-old gesture that expressed more than words.

"Oh, very well," Sheldon Harcourt said in a resigned voice. "Tell your beautiful lady that I shall be honoured if she will dine with me, and I will throttle you, you old villain, if she is ugly or pock-marked!"

"Milor can trust me," *Monsieur* Dessin said, "and you are very gracious."

He bowed low from the waist and with his face wreathed in smiles he went from the room, leaving Sheldon Harcourt with the impression that he had fully intended to have his own way from the start.

'Damn him!' the Englishman thought resentfully. 'I wanted to have a quiet evening alone, so that I could think.'

He had in fact been thinking ever since he had left Paris, but had come to no conclusion. As he sipped his wine he thought that perhaps solitude would only deepen his unavoidable depression.

A few minutes later the door was opened and he turned his head expectantly, only to be considerably surprised.

It was not a woman who stood there, but a small black boy carrying in his arms a silk cushion that was almost bigger than himself.

He was dressed in a long brocade coat which reached to his ankles and was fastened across his chest with gold buttons.

On his head was a turban of peacock-coloured silk with a jewelled brooch at the front which held a feathered egret.

The black boy advanced towards the fire, bowed

courteously to Sheldon Harcourt, and placed his cushion on the arm-chair on the opposite side of the hearth.

Then he bowed again and without speaking went from the room.

Sheldon Harcourt watched him go with amusement.

He was well aware that the aristocratic ladies in France, as in England, thought it *chic* to have a black boy in attendance.

They were there to carry their fans, their gloves, their reticules! Also to run messages and to be on duty at all times of the day and night.

Sheldon Harcourt had often seen weary little black heads nodding, and boys who were little more than babies falling asleep only to be awakened by the sharp slap of a fan or a kick from a pointed shoe.

He noticed that this black boy was not as young as many others he had seen.

In fact, he had the idea as the door closed behind him that he was, despite his height, not so much a boy as a dwarf.

He took another sip of wine as the door opened again.

This time an elderly maid appeared, carrying a rug lined with ermine over her arm, her lace-edged mob-cap very white against a middle-aged face already etched with wrinkles.

She did not, however, cross the room, she merely held the door open and a moment later her mistress appeared.

In fact, Sheldon Harcourt told himself, she made a dramatic entrance and he half-expected to hear a fanfare of trumpets!

Slowly he rose to his feet, noting as he did so that the lady did in fact justify all the adjectives which *Monsieur* Dessin had expended on her.

She was very lovely with dark hair swept back from a widow's peak in the centre of an oval forehead, huge eyes fringed with dark lashes, and a skin which appeared to be dazzlingly white against her black gown.

She was obviously in mourning, but her mourning attire was marked, as only the French could contrive, by an elegance and an allurement which had nothing depressing about it.

She wore rustling black silk with touches of white and a neckline which stopped just short of being immodest.

Slowly, with an elegance and at the same time a dignity, the Vision of Loveliness moved towards Sheldon Harcourt to curtsey to him with a grace which had something regal about it.

His bow in acknowledgement was a model of courtesy.

"*Monsieur,* I am informed by the Proprietor that you are gracious enough to invite me into your private room. I am indeed grateful."

She spoke excellent English, but with a slight accent that had a fascination of its own. Her eyes, when she looked up into his, were as inviting as the smile on her softly curved lips.

"I am delighted to be of service, *Madame,* or should I say *Mademoiselle?*"

"*Je suis la Comtesse* de la Tour," she replied, then gave a little cry and turned angrily towards the maid who was still standing in the open doorway.

"*Fermez la porte,* Francine!" she exclaimed. "If you do not shut the door I shall be overheard, and I shall end up like my poor dear husband—on the guillotine! Why can you not take better care of me?"

"*Pardonnez-moi, Madame!*"

"Give me my rug, then you can go. And remember, do not breathe a word of who I am in this *Hôtel.*"

"*C'est entendu, Madame.*"

The maid brought the ermine rug and laid it on the arm of the chair, then she curtseyed first to her mistress, then to Sheldon Harcourt, and went slowly from the room.

6

"Servants are so stupid, they do not understand," the *Comtesse* said with a gesture of her white hands.

Sheldon Harcourt noticed that she wore a diamond-and-pearl ring over the gold band on her wedding finger.

It complemented an exceptionally fine string of pearls that she wore round her neck and which was her only other adornment.

"You must tell me about yourself, *Comtesse*," he said. "Will you not be seated?"

She sat down on the chair he indicated, pulling out the fullness of her skirts and looking at him tentatively from under her eye-lashes as if she debated whether she should trust him or not.

"I am *Madame* de la Tour," she said after a moment. "Never, never must the word *Comtesse* be spoken while we are on French soil."

She made a sound that was a moan and clasped her hands together.

"My adored husband—I watched him mount the steps to the guillotine! He had committed no crime, save that he was born noble!"

"I am sorry you have suffered in such a way," Sheldon Harcourt said. "May I offer you a glass of wine?"

"Thank you, but I would prefer to wait until dinner is served," the *Comtesse* replied.

"You were telling me about your husband."

"We lived outside Paris at Nogent-sur-Seine. The Revolution seemed far away and did not concern us."

The *Comtesse* put her hands up to her eyes.

"Not . . . at least until a . . . month ago . . . and then . . ."

She seemed to be too overcome with emotion to say any more.

"I understand," Sheldon Harcourt said. "I have also lost many friends."

"You have come from Paris, *Monsieur?*"

"Yes, Paris," he answered, "and I thought things

were a little better until that fool, Barère, demanded the life of the King as an indispensable 'measure of public safety.'"

"*Le pauvre Roi!*" the *Comtesse* murmured. "My heart bleeds for the Queen and her family!"

She paused, then she asked:

"And because the King has been executed, you have to return to England?"

"I certainly had to leave Paris," Sheldon Harcourt replied. "I am convinced, as all Englishmen in France are, that England will declare war on this country."

"But for you it is going home," the *Comtesse* said in a low voice. "For me it is . . . stepping into the . . . unknown."

"You have friends in England?"

"There must be émigrés with whom I am acquainted, but I do not know where they are or how I shall find them."

Sheldon Harcourt looked astonished.

"You are really setting off on this journey all by yourself?"

The *Comtesse* smiled.

"I have Francine, who has looked after me ever since I was a child, and Bobo, who is my personal servant and is far stronger than he looks."

"I thought he might not be as young as he appeared," Sheldon Harcourt remarked.

"You are very observant, *Monsieur!* It is true. Bobo is in fact twenty-five years of age and he is very strong. If anyone attacked me, I swear he would kill them!"

"I am certain that will not happen to you in England," Sheldon Harcourt assured her.

"That is why I am so anxious to get there, to feel safe, to know that your lovely country will welcome me with a warmth that no longer exists in France."

Sheldon Harcourt hoped that she would not be disappointed.

He knew that London was overflowing with refugees and that the initially hospitable attitude of the

English was changing to one of thinly veiled exasperation.

What was more, he had learnt from Englishmen arriving in Paris that the émigrés who fled France at the first sign of what was to come in 1789 called themselves *"Les Purs"* or "the pure ones."

They regarded those who came later almost as if they were traitors because they had stayed so long.

He thought, however, that at least the *Comtesse* did not appear to be impoverished, and for someone who had money and was also beautiful London could be very enjoyable, even if initially she started off without any friends.

Monsieur Dessin, accompanied by two maids and a waiter with the wine, bustled into the room with the first dishes of a long and elaborate meal which was well-cooked and of excellent variety.

The Hôtel d'Angleterre was famous, and the reports of its excellent and expensive table were, Sheldon Harcourt thought, not exaggerated.

The *spécialité de la maison*, fresh sea crabs, was superb, and the champagne was delicious.

There was also the noise from the Dining-Room which came to the ears when the doors were open to remind Sheldon Harcourt continually that he was fortunate to be where he was.

Certainly while they were eating the wind and the storm outside seemed to have grown rougher and at times a sudden gust would blow down the chimney and shake even the sturdy proportions of the Hotel itself.

"It appears we may be marooned here for some time," Sheldon Harcourt remarked.

"I hope not," the *Comtesse* replied.

Then she added quickly:

"That sounds impolite, *Monsieur*, when you have been so kind. But you will understand that I am apprehensive for my own safety."

"I do understand that," Sheldon Harcourt said in his deep voice, "but I think you are quite safe in

9

Calais. The Revolution has not yet travelled far beyond the main cities of France, and the worst crimes have all been committed in Paris."

"It reached Nogent-sur-Seine," the *Comtesse* said with what was almost a sob in her voice.

They had finished dinner and there was only the coffee in front of them and a glass of excellent brandy beside Sheldon Harcourt.

The *Comtesse* put her hand out towards him.

"Will you be kind to me in England, *Monsieur*?" she asked. "You are so distinguished and of such importance that I know with your help and protection I should feel secure."

There was a faint glint of amusement in Sheldon Harcourt's blue eyes.

He was well aware that all through dinner the *Comtesse* was attempting to flirt with him.

He had played his part in the duel of words and glances with an expertise that came from long experience of such encounters with pretty women.

He had half-expected the *Comtesse* to appeal to him as an Englishman for help, but it had in fact come sooner than he had anticipated.

He took her hand as was expected of him and kissed it.

"You must tell me a little more about yourself," he said.

For a moment her fingers pressed his, then they escaped from his hold like a butterfly flitting away into the sunshine.

"What do you wish to know?" she asked. "My husband was a rich man, but I am not certain how much I can . . . salvage from his . . . estate."

"You have money in England?"

"I am . . . not sure. When I reach London, I must visit Attorneys and make . . . enquiries. In the meantime, I have enough to live . . . comfortably."

Just for a moment her fingers went to the string of pearls round her neck and the diamonds in her ring seemed to flash at him.

"If you would advise me, *Monsieur,* at which Hotel I should stay when I reach London, then I can look for accommodation, and of course a fashionable address."

She gave a little sigh.

"If only I could stay with . . . someone until I have time to look . . . round."

A smile twisted Sheldon Harcourt's lips.

"I regret I am not in a position to invite you to my family Mansion," he said. "But I will certainly do my best to find you a suitable place to rest until you can choose a house to suit you."

"You do not know what it is like, *Monsieur,*" she replied with a little throb of emotion in her voice, "to be alone in the world . . . to have no-one to care for one . . . no-one to love."

"I have already said how sorry I am."

"You are very kind. Perhaps if I were a little older, a little more experienced, it would be easier; but my husband did everything for me—everything!"

"And now you are alone. It is a very sad story."

"I try to be brave—as he was brave when he climbed the steps to the guillotine and said, his voice ringing out: 'God take my soul, and the devil keep yours!'"

As if the repetition of the words was too much for the *Comtesse,* she put her hands up to her face.

"A little cognac," Sheldon Harcourt suggested, pouring some from the decanter into a glass.

The *Comtesse* shook her head as he said:

"I am sure you have been very brave until now. But it would be a mistake to give way, however tragic your memories. Courage!"

"Courage is what I shall need in the . . . future," the *Comtesse* said softly.

She took her hands from her eyes and said:

"The English are always so brave. It is the fortitude which exists in their very blood!"

"You are very complimentary, *Madame!*"

"Are you . . . surprised?"

11

Now the flirtatious look was back in her dark eyes and picking up her glass she raised it.

"You are an extremely kind and handsome *gentil-homme!*"

Sheldon Harcourt bowed but he did not toast his companion in return. Instead, he sat back in his chair, very much at his ease, watching her.

She was certainly very lovely. Even on closer inspection her skin was perfect and her features were delicate and very aristocratic.

A little straight nose between large and eloquent eyes, the tiny pointed chin, and the perfect pearly teeth glinting between her red lips were all part of a picture of beauty that was accentuated by her grace.

As if she realised that she was being scrutinised, the *Comtesse* flushed a little.

"You look as if . . . how do you say in England? That you are 'summing me up,' " she said.

"Your English is astounding!" Sheldon Harcourt exclaimed. "How did you learn to speak so fluently?"

"It is quite simple . . . my mother was English!"

"That accounts for it, but in fact you look very French."

"I take after my father and have always lived in France, but I have longed . . . yes, I have always longed to visit the country which my mother called home and of which she spoke with such emotion."

"Then you have relatives in England!"

The *Comtesse* spread wide her hands.

"I may have . . . I do not know."

She dropped her eyes as she said:

"My mother ran away with my father. It was a *mésalliance* for the son of an aristocratic family. It had been intended that his marriage should be arranged, as are all marriages in France, but he was a rebel!"

She smiled and her eyes seemed to sparkle as she said:

"So you understand, *Monsieur*, why I am here."

"I understand, and shall I say that I am very glad that you are?"

12

"I meant in the world . . . not in this private room at this . . . particular moment," the *Comtesse* pouted.

"I am well aware what you meant," Sheldon Harcourt said, "but I was speaking entirely selfishly. I am glad that a stormy sea and even the horrors of a Revolution have brought us together!"

"You are very kind and very . . . flattering."

Her eye-lashes were dark against her pale cheeks as she rose from the table and moved towards the fire.

As she stood for a moment, holding out her fingers to the blaze, the flames brought out blue and purple lights in her dark hair and left a gleam like a small star in the centre of her eyes.

Sheldon Harcourt rose to join her.

"I must retire to bed," the *Comtesse* said. "It has been a long day and I am fatigued."

"Let us hope the wind will drop and we can make the crossing tomorrow."

"And if we do, I shall see you again?"

"I hope so."

"I want to see you. Can you not understand that I want to see you very much?"

She looked up at him and his eyes narrowed.

Then without speaking he put out his arms and drew her against him.

She made no resistance; in fact, her head fell back naturally against his shoulder, as his mouth came down on hers.

Her lips were very soft beneath his and he felt a quiver run through her.

His kiss became more insistent, more demanding, and his arms tightened until it was hard for her to breathe.

Then as her hands fluttered as if she would struggle against him, he raised his head and said in a very different tone from the one he had used before:

"Now, suppose you tell me the truth?"

"The . . . truth?"

Her eyes were dark and very wide as she stared at him.

13

"The truth!" he repeated.

"W-what ... do you mean?"

"You are not the *Comtesse* de la Tour!"

"H-how ... do you ... know?"

"I have met the *Comtesse* and she is in fact middle-aged and a plain woman."

"That is ... unfortunate!"

"Very! And there is something else I would like you to explain."

"What is that?"

"Why you are wearing a wedding ring? I am sure you are not married. You have certainly never been kissed before."

The woman Sheldon Harcourt was holding in his arms made a quick movement and was free of him.

"*Tiens!*" she exclaimed. "What did I do that was wrong?"

"Not wrong," Sheldon Harcourt corrected. "Shall we say you are a trifle inexperienced."

"Would anyone be able to ... tell?"

"Perhaps not."

She stamped her foot.

"Then why should you be able to find me out? It is unfortunate, is it not, that of all the men who might have been in this room tonight, it had to be you!"

She paused, then added as if in afterthought:

"And you also met the *Comtesse* de la Tour ... before she died under the guillotine."

Sheldon Harcourt smiled because she sounded so exasperated, almost like a small kitten spitting at the world.

"Suppose you sit down and tell me what this is all about?"

He thought she hesitated. Then as if she made up her mind to trust him she sat down in the chair and pulled the ermine rug over her knees.

"What ... do you want to ... know?" she asked in a rather small voice.

"The truth! You have made me curious."

14

"If I tell you the truth, *Monsieur*, will you help me?"

"That depends on what you want or what you expect of me."

"You are English, a nobleman, and you are rich—yes?"

Sheldon Harcourt laughed and poured himself out another glass of brandy, then sat down in the chair opposite her.

"We are certainly starting off at cross-purposes," he said. "You have only one thing right. I am English, but I am not a nobleman. My 'title' exists only in the imagination of *Monsieur* Dessin, and I have scarcely a sou with which to bless myself."

"*Hélas!* Is that true?"

"Completely and absolutely true," he answered. "I am returning to England more like an émigré than you, my dear, so you cannot rely upon me to be of much assistance to you in your predicament, if that is what it is."

"It is worse!"

"Tell me," he said. "I have been frank with you and I expect you to be equally frank with me."

"It is true I am not married," the woman sitting opposite him began, "but I thought it would be *pas convenable* and not very impressive to arrive in London with only Francine and Bobo to chaperon me. A widow would not need one."

"You knew the de la Tours?"

"Mama and I lived in the same village but they did not speak to us. We were beneath their condescension."

"Why?"

There was a slight hesitation, as if she chose her words with care. Then as if she decided to hide nothing she answered:

"My father was the *Duc* de Valence. He loved my mother and my mother loved him. He had been married, long before they met, to a dull, unimaginative

15

woman who preferred her Church and the company of her Priests to that of her husband."

"So you are a love-child."

He thought as he looked at her that it would account for her beauty, just as there was no mistaking her noble ancestry in every line of her features and every movement of her body.

"The *Duc* died in Paris last . . . August."

There was no doubt now of the throb of anguish behind her words.

"I remember, he was one of the twelve hundred aristocrats and Bishops who lost their lives in the massacre," Sheldon Harcourt said.

"Mama could not live without him," the young voice went on. "She just seemed to fade away and . . . die."

There was a little sob.

"I buried her two weeks before . . . Christmas."

"So you are alone."

She fought for control before she answered his question.

"Completely alone, except for Francine and Bobo."

Now he could understand why there would be no friends waiting for her in London, no relations to open their doors to the daughter of a French *Duc*.

"What do you intend to do?" he asked.

"I intend to get married!"

"Get married?"

"Of course! I wish to be respectable."

There was a note of steel now in her voice and it was difficult for Sheldon Harcourt to suppress the smile that twisted the corners of his lips.

"It might be easier for you to find a protector."

She sat bolt upright in her chair and her eyes flashed at him.

"Do you think that is what I want? Do you not think I have suffered enough from being sneered at, slighted, and despised because my father could not give my mother a wedding ring?"

She drew in her breath.

"I intend to be rich. I intend to have a position in life. I intend to be respectable and no-one . . . no-one shall stop me!"

She almost spat the words at him and after a moment of surprise he leant back in his chair and laughed.

"You are magnificent! If anyone can achieve what they set out to do, it will be you!"

"And you will help me?"

"How can I?"

"You can tell me where to go. You can introduce me to men of the right sort. You have no money, you say, but influence and knowing the right people are more important than wealth."

She paused.

"We will make a bargain—*oui?* You help me and I will help you. I will marry a rich man . . . we share his money!"

Again Sheldon Harcourt laughed.

"You are incorrigible! I have never had such a fantastic proposition put to me."

"Why is it so fantastic?"

"Do you really think I would agree to take your money?"

Her eyes narrowed for a moment.

"Why not?" she asked. "You say you are not noble, but you are a gentleman. My father would have approved of you. You cannot pretend that you would not be accepted in Society and in many important houses in England."

Sheldon Harcourt did not answer.

His eyes were watching her and she had a feeling that he was thinking over what she was saying.

"We will arrive in London together," the soft voice continued. "You tell your friends you have befriended me, that you are looking after me because my husband . . . who died on the guillotine . . . was your friend."

She smiled.

"One introduction will lead to another, and once I

17

have found a man who is rich enough to be my husband I will marry him!"

She threw herself back in her chair.

"It is quite easy. Where are the difficulties?"

"What is your name . . . your real name?" Sheldon Harcourt asked.

"Cerissa," she answered, "and the only other name to which I am entitled is my mother's, which is Waring, but we never used it."

"Then what did you call yourselves?"

"Valence! Why not? I was not ashamed of my father."

"Why should you be?"

She gave him a quick glance.

"Do you mean that?"

"Of course I mean it. It is not your fault that your parents were unable to be united by the Church!"

Cerissa gave a sigh.

"They were united in every other way. They adored each other. They were two people who were meant to be together since the beginning of time."

She made a little gesture with her hands.

"Perhaps they are together now . . . who knows?"

There was something spiritual in her dark eyes as she spoke and she looked very young.

Then as Sheldon Harcourt did not speak she looked at him anxiously and said:

"I have told you the truth. Will you help me?"

"Perhaps. I am thinking."

"Then let me think with you."

She thrust aside the ermine rug and threw herself on her knees beside him.

"Please help me," she pleaded. "I knew as soon as I came into this room that you were the sort of Englishman I wanted to find and that you were someone I could trust."

"You really think you can trust a penniless adventurer?" he asked. "Because that is what I am. I have lived on my wits for the last five years."

18

She was still for a moment, then she said:

"You had to leave England?"

"Yes, I had to come abroad," he said.

There was a finality in his tone which told her not to probe any further.

"And now that you are going back . . . may I not go with you?"

"I really cannot see how I can be of any use to you. Besides, a beautiful widow would doubtless fare better without a male companion, who would cause a great deal of comment and gossip."

"Then perhaps it would be better for me not to be married," Cerissa said. "It was actually Francine's idea."

Sheldon Harcourt stared down at the little heart-shaped face raised to his.

"Listen," he said, "no-one, once they knew you, would credit that you are a married woman."

"Why not? I thought I acted the part so . . . well."

"Not really," he answered. "Not well enough to deceive anyone who is experienced in the ways of the world."

She pouted very prettily before she said:

"Then I will be a *jeune fille*. It will not be difficult to be what I am."

"How old are you?"

"A little over eighteen."

"It is very young."

"I feel very old," she said with a sigh. "So much has happened. I have been so unhappy. I must learn to look after myself."

She sounded like a child protesting that she was not afraid of the dark.

"The great art of disguise," Sheldon Harcourt said, "is to be natural. To be, if possible, one's self. Let me think . . ."

He stared into the fire for a moment before he asked:

"Did any of the Valence family become émigrés?"

"None of them. My father said that only cowards

19

ran away, and he was a Frenchman. If he had to die, then he would die on French soil!"

Again there was a little sob in her voice as she said:

"And that is what he ... did!"

"And the *Duchesse?*"

"They guillotined her with her favourite Bishop. I think it was poetic justice, as she loved him so much!"

Sheldon Harcourt put out his fingers to touch Cerissa's cheek.

"You are a blood-thirsty little thing!"

"*J'ai détesté cette femme*—I hated her!" Cerissa answered fiercely. "She said cruel and unkind things about Mama. She tried in every way possible to make our lives intolerable."

"I expect she was jealous."

"If she lost her husband it was her own fault! She made no effort to attract him. I heard Papa say once: '*Mon Dieu!* The intolerable boredom of my honeymoon!'"

"And yet you wish to be married?"

"Of course I wish to be married! I want people to respect me, to admire me; I want an *entrée* to all the great houses which have always closed their doors to me."

She drew in her breath.

"Can you imagine what it was like to see Papa dressed in all his finery leaving for dinner at the Palace of the Tuileries or a Ball at Versailles, and know that Mama must be left behind?"

There was a pause before she went on:

"He would talk to us of the people he met, of the Statesmen with whom he talked, the conversations he had with the King and Queen."

Cerissa gave a little sigh.

"I knew as I listened that I should always be ... outside the right doors ... never ... inside them."

She put out both her hands to take Sheldon Harcourt's in hers.

"Help me, and, however much you may laugh, I swear I will help you. You say that you are an adventurer . . . well, I am an adventuress. Why can we not work together?"

"Robbing the rich?" Sheldon Harcourt asked mockingly.

"All we want is one rich man . . . just one . . . who will offer me marriage."

Cerissa jumped to her feet.

"Look at me! Look and tell me there is not one single man in the whole of England foolish enough to lay his heart at my feet!"

She looked exquisite in the firelight—like a comet burning across the sky.

"He should not be—difficult to . . . find," Sheldon Harcourt admitted, as if the words were dragged from him.

"Then find him!" Cerissa ordered. "Find him, and our fortunes are made . . . both yours and mine!"

"It is not as easy as that!"

"Why not?"

"Because, looking as you do, people will be suspicious if I am constantly in your company."

"*Tiens!* That I can understand! I know only too well what was said about Mama, but . . ."

She paused suddenly and her eyes lit up.

"Why should you not be my Guardian? Supposing Papa, as he went up the steps to the guillotine, committed me to your charge, saying:

"'This is my child whom I love. Protect her and keep her safe. Take her to England where her life will not be in danger!'"

Cerissa spoke dramatically, then she asked:

"If Papa had said that to you, what would you have replied?"

"If I had been so foolish as to be standing round the guillotine waiting for trouble," Sheldon Harcourt answered, "I presume I would have found it difficult to refuse the last request of a man who was about to die."

21

"There you are, you see!" Cerissa exclaimed triumphantly. "That is our story. You are my Guardian . . ."

She stopped and put her head to one side.

"You look *almost* old enough to be a Guardian."

"I am thirty-one," Sheldon Harcourt replied. "I dare say no-one would ask to see my birth certificate if I added a few years to my age."

"Very well. You shall be thirty-seven!" Cerissa said. "That is old enough in all conscience!"

"Very old," he said sarcastically, "to someone as young as you!"

"I will be . . . seventeen," Cerissa announced. "After all, that is what I was a little over a year ago. I have not altered much since then. I will make myself look young . . . very young. This hair-style is too mature. Francine thought it suitable for a married woman."

She pulled her rings off her fingers as she spoke and handed the pearl-and-diamond one to Sheldon Harcourt.

"Sooner or later you will have to see what price you can get for that and eventually Mama's pearl necklace will have to go too."

"You are very trusting. Supposing I abscond with this ring and you never see me again?"

"I trust you, and my instinct is never at fault where people are concerned. Papa often said that I had the makings of a witch!"

"I hope your witchcraft is working overtime at the moment," Sheldon Harcourt remarked. "A crazier, more hare-brained scheme I have never heard outside the door of a play-house."

"An actress! That is what I shall be!" Cerissa cried. "And you will produce me, just as if I were on the stage. *La Comtesse* Cerissa de Valence! It has a romantic ring to it, *n'est-ce pas!*"

"You have not told me how many children the *Duc* had."

"Three," Cerissa answered, "or rather originally

there were five, but two died. The daughter was ugly, like her mother. He never liked her!"

"What happened to her and the two sons?"

"They were in the same prison as my father. It was believed locally that they were executed with him. At any rate, not one of the family came back to the *Château* . . . before it was looted . . . of that I am sure!"

"The *Duc's* property was near your mother's house?"

"About three miles away. That is why he brought my mother and me to Nogent-sur-Seine. He preferred to live in the country and he spent most of his time with us. When he went to Paris we went with him. He gave my mother an apartment not far from his magnificent Mansion."

Cerissa made a sound of disgust.

"A little apartment . . . a tiny country house . . . always hidden away! That is the story of my life . . . to feel ashamed and insignificant!"

She crossed the room restlessly, then returned to the fire.

"That is why I intend to be respectable, to drive to Church in a carriage, to be shown into the front pew, and to entertain the right people."

"You will find them very dull!"

"Nothing that is right and proper can be dull to me. I have known enough of the other sort of life."

Cerissa drew in her breath before she went on:

"I have seen my mother wince when people insulted her. I have heard the contempt even in the tradesmen's voices for a *chère amie* . . . a woman who in most people's eyes has nothing to recommend her . . . except that she has a man to pay her bills."

There was a note in Cerissa's voice which was almost venomous. Then once again she flung herself down on her knees beside Sheldon Harcourt.

"Help me! Oh, please help me! This is my only chance—the only opportunity I am ever likely to have to find security, to be the person I want to be."

She was very beautiful and the pleading in her eyes was irresistible. But surprisingly Sheldon Harcourt's blue eyes were hard and there was nothing sympathetic about his tone as he said:

"If I do help you, will you obey me?"

"You mean that you will . . . agree to . . . introduce me to . . . England?"

"I think perhaps I am making the greatest mistake I have ever made in my life," Sheldon Harcourt replied. "There is an adage I have always followed which says: 'He travels fastest who travels alone.'"

"Nevertheless, you will . . . travel with me?"

"I presume I shall have to," he answered, "but only if you swear on all you hold sacred that if I find you the right husband you will marry him and be prepared to take the consequences, whatever they may be."

Cerissa gave a sigh of relief which came from the very depths of her body.

"I swear!" she cried. "Oh, *Monsieur, je vous remercie!* I thank you!"

Chapter Two

"I think we should pool our resources and see how much we have to spend," Sheldon Harcourt suggested.

They were sitting in the private room in the Hotel.

While the wind outside was still blowing hard, the sea was dropping and he anticipated that by the next day the ship would be able to sail.

He had not suggested that Cerissa should accompany him when he walked that morning to the Quay to find the sailors on the cross-Channel packet staring gloomily at the waves breaking over the jetty.

When the wind stood fair, Dover could be reached from Calais in about three hours, but if the sea was rough it would often take five to six.

At the beginning of the century the cross-Channel ships had been rough, uncomfortable, and very often unseaworthy, but now conditions were far better. There were even two private cabins aboard the *Queen Anne*, on which Sheldon Harcourt had booked their passage.

He engaged one of them, impressed upon the Captain the importance of himself and the *Comtesse*, then returned to the Hotel.

There was nothing attractive in the town of Calais, which consisted of a few narrow streets which ran into a central market-place.

The houses were low and looked poor and bleak. Sheldon Harcourt reckoned that there could not be more than five to six thousand inhabitants in the town.

But in compensation there was something very pleasing in the manner and appearance of the people. Despite the tales of aggression and the frequent rudeness encountered in the rest of France, Sheldon Harcourt found that they were vastly obliging.

The rain had stopped and a pale sun was trying to force its way between the grey clouds.

He noticed that there were quite a number of pretty women amongst the fisher-wives wearing their red petticoats and heavy sabots. Many of them had fair hair and blue eyes.

He had been told when visiting France in the past that when Edward III had captured Calais he had turned out all the French inhabitants and replaced them with English citizens.

It was therefore not surprising that English travellers arriving at the French Port felt that they were welcomed in the streets and shops by their own kith and kin.

Sheldon Harcourt had long known that the English, especially the aristocrats, when going abroad for the first time believed that the French were "debauched and irreligious" and were all extremely garrulous.

There were few of his contemporaries in the London Clubs who were not prepared to state categorically that the French were "a grasping race, none too clean," and that "when they are not behaving like actors they are acting like monkeys."

They had not listened to him before he left England and he was quite certain that no-one would listen to him now when he returned.

But speaking after five years in France, he found the ordinary people far from being the blackguards they were supposed to be, had in fact a quick understanding and were courteous and friendly.

He remembered with a smile how during an argument in Paris with a somewhat disagreeable English visitor he had said that in his opinion the men were "masters of good breeding" and the women "fascinating and at times irresistible."

His opinion, he thought now, was certainly confirmed by Cerissa.

Sitting in front of the fire, she looked exceedingly beautiful, and at the same time he found her outstandingly intelligent. She told him that she had been well educated.

"Papa hated stupid women," Cerissa said.

"You attended a school or a convent?"

Cerissa shook her head.

"The sort of place where I should have liked to be educated would certainly not have accepted me," she said. "I might have contaminated the other girls!"

There was a bitterness in her voice that was always there when she spoke of her experience as the illegitimate daughter of the *Duc*.

Sheldon Harcourt changed the conversation.

But he thought now as he looked at her that it was easy to understand her resentment.

Despite her youth and her obvious innocence, which made it impossible for her to act with the sophistication of an experienced married woman, she had a poise which was unmistakable.

It came, Sheldon Harcourt thought, from constant association with a man who was as cultured and intelligent as the *Duc* must have been.

He had also learnt that Cerissa's mother came from a good English County family who had been accepted in Court circles.

It had been in fact at Buckingham Palace that Madelaine Waring had met the *Duc* de Valence.

He had asked to be introduced to the prettiest girl he could see at the State Ball and after one dance had lost his heart.

Colonel Sir Archibald Waring had brought his wife and daughter to London for the Season.

The *Duc* had called on Lady Waring the following day and been received with some coolness.

Madelaine's mother was well aware of the reason

for the *Duc*'s visit and was not in the least impressed by the attentions of a French aristocrat with a wife and family at home in France.

But it was impossible for the *Duc* and Madelaine to be kept apart.

Notes were passed between them secretly, with a servant inevitably becoming *le complice de l'amour*.

They met clandestinely and when the *Duc* returned to France Madelaine went with him!

Looking at Cerissa, it was not hard to understand the *Duc*'s infatuation if the mother had been as lovely as the daughter.

It was, however, extraordinary, Sheldon Harcourt thought to himself, how a woman could change her appearance overnight.

Gone was the sophisticated elegance of the young widow whom Cerissa had impersonated when she had first entered the private room.

In her place was a very young girl looking at life with enchanted eyes, her dark hair curling softly round her cheeks.

Her fichu was crossed modestly over her breast and allowed an onlooker little more than a peep of the dazzlingly white skin at the base of her long neck.

"There is one thing which is fortunate," Sheldon Harcourt said, following the train of his own thoughts. "You will not require to purchase many gowns."

"That is true," Cerissa agreed. "I have all Mama's wardrobe. As she always wished to appear quiet and unassuming, she usually wore black."

She gave a little smile as she added:

"As a matter of fact, because she was fair it became her better than anything else."

Sheldon Harcourt did not speak and Cerissa glanced down at her own black skirt.

"I prefer gay colours, but as I must appear sad and in mourning, Francine will add touches of white to Mama's gowns to make them look younger, and later I can wear white with a black sash."

"Appearances are important," Sheldon Harcourt

remarked, "but we will still need money, and, if we are to set out together on this wild adventure, at least we had best know where we stand."

His voice was uncompromising as he said:

"As far as I am concerned, my worldly goods consist of the equivalent of sixty pounds in English money."

"That will be enough," Cerissa answered, "with what I have."

She saw his lips tighten and knew that he disliked more than he would say the thought of taking her money.

She reached out to put her hand on his arm.

"Your chief asset, *cher Monsieur,* is yourself," she said softly. "Your knowledge of England and the social friends you will make are of inestimable value."

"You are very sure of me," Sheldon Harcourt answered, "and yet you know nothing about my past, present, or future."

"I know everything that is important," Cerissa answered, with a little sideways glance from under her eye-lids.

"Let us get down to hard facts," he said sharply.

"Very well," Cerissa replied. "My Papa gave my mother half a million francs when the Revolution started. He put it in a Bank in Paris in the name of 'Madelaine Waring,' and said: 'This is for you and Cerissa if anything should happen to me.'"

"A Bank in Paris!" Sheldon Harcourt repeated.

"Mama put most of her jewellery there too when we left for the country. We often talked of going back to collect some of it, but we were afraid."

"I can understand that."

"When I decided to go to England," Cerissa went on, "I thought of writing to the Bank to transfer the money to London. Then when things became worse I doubted if any letter posted from Nogent-sur-Seine would ever reach Paris."

"And now, if war is declared," Sheldon Harcourt said, "the money will undoubtedly be frozen."

"You mean . . . I shall never . . . get it?"

"Not until the war is over."

"I was afraid of that. If only I had been brave enough to go to Paris . . . but when I thought of what . . . happened to Papa . . ."

She gave a little shudder and the fear in her eyes was very evident.

"Perhaps it will prove to be a nest-egg for your old age," Sheldon Harcourt said optimistically. "What else do you possess?"

"When Papa was alive he gave Mama large sums of money regularly every month with which to pay for our food and clothes and the wages of the servants. There were others besides Francine and Bobo."

"And that money, of course, ceased last August."

Cerissa nodded.

"Mama dismissed the other servants, but even so, I had to pay the Doctor, and of course . . . the funeral."

"What have you left?" Sheldon Harcourt asked quietly.

"I have about seventy-five hundred francs."

"Three hundred pounds in English money. That is, if we get a good rate of exchange across the Channel, which I rather doubt."

"I have also Mama's pearl necklace which I was wearing last night, her ring, and the diamond brooch."

She gave a little sigh.

"She had such beautiful jewels. If only we had been sensible enough to keep them with us instead of leaving them in Paris."

"It is always easy to be wise after the event," Sheldon Harcourt said, "and regrets are a complete waste of time."

"You are right," Cerissa agreed. "Also the furniture in the house was very valuable. Papa wanted Mama to have a setting worthy of her beauty."

"What did you do about the furniture?"

"Francine and I packed up everything we could and asked the Doctor who had attended Papa and who had been fond of him to store it for me."

"And the house?"

"We locked the door and left late at night so that no one should see us go."

Cerissa made a helpless movement with her hands.

"It may now be burnt to the ground as the rabble burnt the *Château!*"

There was a note of pain in her voice but she continued:

"I brought away with me a few *objets d'art*. Little gold boxes set with jewels, miniatures which Papa gave Mama because he said many of the faces resembled her own!"

She was silent as if remembering, before she went on:

"There are some which she treasured particularly as they were presents at Christmas and anniversaries, many of those are made in gold and ornamented with precious stones."

"You must not sell them until you are absolutely desperate!" Sheldon Harcourt said firmly.

He knew without being told that they were all that Cerissa had as a background, all that was left to remind her of her mother.

At the same time, although what she possessed sounded like a lot, he knew only too well how easily money could disappear. Her three hundred pounds would not last forever.

"I have a proposition to put to you," he said after a moment.

Cerissa did not speak but she raised her eyes to his.

"It is that when we arrive in England we do not proceed to London," he said. "For one thing, I have personal reasons for not wishing to be seen there, for another it would serve our purpose and undoubtedly be cheaper if we went to Bath."

"Bath?" Cerissa repeated quickly. "I think I have heard Mama speak of it."

"It is a fashionable Spa in the west of England

where at this time of the year great numbers of the aristocrats go to improve their health and enjoy its mild climate."

Cerissa was listening intently as he went on:

"Bath is in fact a very elegant and attractive city. As it is smaller than London, it will be far easier for you to meet the nobility without formality. Besides, I have always believed on principle that it is best to be 'a big fish in a small pond.'"

He smiled a little wryly as he added:

"Not a very pretty simile for anyone as dazzling as you!"

"Do you think I am dazzling?" Cerissa asked, her head tilted a little to one side.

"I am sure you will be the star of the Assembly-Rooms and the Balls which are attended by all the *jeunesse dorée* and everyone of any consequence."

"Then let us go to Bath," Cerissa exclaimed excitedly.

"I will write a letter reserving rooms, which can be posted the moment we set foot in Dover," Sheldon Harcourt said. "It will be a long and tiring journey across country, especially at this time of the year, but once we arrive I am certain it will be worth the effort."

"I am prepared to do anything you suggest," Cerissa said meekly.

"What I am also going to suggest," Sheldon Harcourt answered, "is that you allow me to change your money here in France into English pounds."

Cerissa looked surprised and he went on:

"I have the feeling that our host, *Monsieur* Dessin, has often been forced to accept a large number of pounds from English travellers arriving and departing."

"Of course," she murmured.

"With the threat of war looming over him," Sheldon Harcourt continued, "he will be worried as to how he will be able to get rid of them."

"That is very clever of you!" Cerissa said admiringly. "I will run upstairs and get my money. I know where Francine has hidden it."

She jumped to her feet as she spoke, eager to do something.

Sheldon Harcourt was well aware that at the back of her mind there was always the fear that if they delayed very much longer something would prevent her from leaving France.

She came back with a great handful of francs, gave them to him, and said:

"I have brought you everything I possess."

"As I said before," he remarked, "you are very trusting."

"I am trusting you with something far more important than money," Cerissa answered, ". . . myself!"

"I am already aware that it is a very grave responsibility!"

He spoke mockingly, but there was a different expression in his eyes as he looked down at her. Then abruptly he went from the room, shutting the door behind him.

Cerissa sat down on the hearth-rug in front of the fire.

"I am grateful for that man," she said in her heart. "I know he will look after me and keep me safe. I never make a mistake. What is more, I think Mama and Papa would have liked him. He is *très gentil.*"

She sat staring into the flames as if she saw pictures in them.

* * *

The waves were still white-crested but the sea was nevertheless subsiding.

The sun had swept away the clouds, and the wind, although it was still blowing, could no longer be described as a gale.

There was no doubt that Cerissa and her entourage were causing a sensation amongst the other passengers waiting to board the *Queen Anne.*

Never had they imagined that anyone embarking on a sea voyage could in the first place look so elegant.

Instead of their heavy shawls, capes, coats, and scarves, Cerissa wore a travelling cloak of black velvet lined and edged with chinchilla.

The soft grey fur framed her small face enchantingly, and her smiling red lips and dark-fringed sparkling eyes made the tedious wait for embarkation seem an adventure rather than an acute discomfort.

The eyes of the spectators wandered from Cerissa to Sheldon Harcourt.

By contrast he seemed abnormally big and tall; his fashionable coat was exceedingly smart, as were his shining boots, which seemed to reflect like mirrors the tumult round him.

As if these two outstandingly attractive and handsome people were not entertainment enough, the servants who accompanied them and who were in charge of the great mound of luggage were equally sensational.

Francine, her face framed by the white ruchings inside her severe bonnet, looked grim and awe-inspiring, while Bobo was a joke!

Wearing a fantastic claret-coloured livery plenteously bespattered with gold buttons, he gave orders to the porters in a shrill authoritative tone which surprisingly made them obey him.

Sheldon Harcourt noted with amusement that the buttons on Bobo's coat bore the coronet and crest of the *Duc* de Valence, and he saw too that more of the baggage was engraved in the same manner.

He did not ask the question but Cerissa was aware of it, for she said in a low voice that only he could hear:

"Bobo joined the mob who were looting my father's *Château*."

"Which would account for the buttons on his livery!" Sheldon Harcourt remarked.

"I am entitled to them," Cerissa said fiercely.

He did not contradict her.

He only watched with a twinkle in his eyes the

way her chin went up, and she seemed to carry herself a few inches higher when she thought of the position that she felt should by right have been hers.

But if Cerissa wished to be married and respectable, Sheldon Harcourt had discovered that Francine was rigidly determined that nothing whatever should prevent it.

He had realised the first day after they met that Francine was regarding him with eyes that unmistakably expressed anger and that the manner in which she spoke was abrupt to the point of rudeness.

"What is wrong with your maid?" he asked Cerissa when Francine, having brought to the private room something her mistress required, flounced out in a manner that was markedly aggressive.

Cerissa smiled.

"Francine thinks that you cannot·be as important or as grand as you appear, since you are travelling without a valet. She also points out that it is unnatural that someone as handsome as you should remain a bachelor if he had any money with which to keep a wife!"

Sheldon Harcourt threw back his head and laughed.

"Francine is very astute!"

"I have explained to her that you will assist me to attain respectability, but she does not believe me. She knows how I have suffered but she is afraid I will lose my heart!"

Cerissa made an expressive gesture with her hands.

"For Mama it was different. She loved Papa and she was completely and absolutely happy when they were together; but as for me . . . I was the odd one out!"

"Outside the door even in your own home!" Sheldon Harcourt teased.

"You laugh . . . but it is true!"

"I am not laughing unkindly," he said. "I understand exactly what you felt, and that is why, if it is in my power, I will help you pick the ripest peach from the very top of the social tree."

"I think perhaps you had better convince Francine that this is your intention, otherwise she may prevail upon Bobo to injure you!"

Sheldon Harcourt looked surprised.

"Bobo can be dangerous," Cerissa explained. "When they were looting the *Château* he half-killed a man who tried to take away from him something belonging to my Papa which he thought I would like to have."

"He must be careful. If he behaves like that in England he will end up in prison!"

"I have told him so . . . but where you are concerned it is best that Francine realises that you are my friend . . . and that you do not . . . intend to be . . . my lover."

"So that is what they suspect!" Sheldon Harcourt said. "It is really not surprising."

Cerissa put her head a little to one side.

"Would you . . . like to be my . . . lover?"

Sheldon Harcourt brought his fist down sharply on the table in front of him so that the ink-pot rattled.

"That is the sort of question you should not ask. You are my Ward, I am your Guardian, and very much older than you. You will treat me with respect!"

"Even when we are alone?" Cerissa asked.

"Always! At all times," he replied. "To act a part you must think yourself into it. You must *be* it. One slip—one unconscious slip—could give the whole game away."

He looked at her severely as he said:

"From now on we play our parts twenty-four hours a day. We never relax, we never step out of them, not even for one second."

Cerissa smiled at him flirtatiously before she said beguilingly:

"*C'est entendu.* Before we . . . begin, may I just

36

... say, *merci, mon brave?* And add that I think you are ... very attractive and very ... handsome!"

"Thank you," Sheldon Harcourt answered. "And may I in return tell you that your hair is untidy and you have a smut on the end of your nose?"

"Ma foi!"

Cerissa sprang to her feet and rushed to stand in front of a mirror which was hanging on the wall.

She scrutinised her reflection for a second, then she turned round to say:

"It is not true! You said that merely to provoke me!"

"Merely to show you the difference in our positions," Sheldon Harcourt said. "Now we must decide on how you will address me."

"I have already thought of that," Cerissa answered. "I think '*Mon Gardieu*' sounds too formal. I shall call you '*Monseigneur.*' It has a much more attractive ring to it!"

"That is used in addressing Royalty, Bishops, or at least someone as important as your father."

"And ... where I am concerned ... you are as important as he ... was," Cerissa said softly.

"Very well, then, *Monseigneur,*" Sheldon Harcourt agreed. "And do not forget!"

His voice was sharp, he had the suspicion that Cerissa was laughing at him and he was annoyed.

He had an opportunity of speaking to Francine that evening when she brought Cerissa's cushion and rug to the private room before dinner.

Sheldon Harcourt knew by the set of her shoulders and the tight line of her lips that she was suspicious of him.

"I want to talk to you, Francine."

He spoke in French even though he was well aware that she understood English.

Francine straightened herself and stood looking at him, her hands folded correctly in front of her.

She was stiff and unbending, Sheldon Harcourt thought, just the type of maid that Cerissa should have in attendance on her.

"When we arrive in England," he said aloud, "I am taking your mistress with me to Bath. She knows no-one in my country, and I hope to introduce her to the right Society, where she will find a husband who will look after her and protect her in the future."

Francine did not move, there was just a glint in her eyes which told Sheldon Harcourt that he had aroused a response in her.

She did not speak and he went on:

"You know better than anyone else how little money *Mademoiselle* has, and what a short time it will last. But she is very beautiful and at Bath she will meet a great number of eligible bachelors, one of whom I am quite convinced will prove a suitable *parti* for such an attractive young woman."

"You mean her to marry, *Monsieur?* You swear it?"

"I am not deceiving you, Francine," Sheldon Harcourt said. "*Mademoiselle* has told me that you did not believe her. Well, you can believe me! I have no designs upon your mistress. I wish only to be her friend."

Francine's eyes searched Sheldon Harcourt's face as if seeking the truth; then she made a little sound that was almost a sob as she said:

"I would die for *M'mselle* Cerissa, *Monsieur!* I have been with her since she was born. She is more to me than if she were my own child."

"Then we must work together for her good," Sheldon Harcourt said. "I shall require the assistance of both you and Bobo. Is that clear?"

Francine knew exactly what he was saying without his putting it into words.

She dropped him a curtsey and it was more respectful than any she had hitherto accorded him.

"We will help you, *Monsieur. Le Bon Dieu* has sent you to our assistance."

There was a note of sincerity in Francine's voice which prevented Sheldon Harcourt from smiling as she left the room.

He had thought to himself as he spoke to her that

the whole thing was too like the Cheltenham Theatricals to be real, and he laughed at himself for taking part in it. At the same time, the whole set-up intrigued him.

He knew as he stepped aboard the *Queen Anne* that he was looking forward to what lay ahead and was in a very different mood from the one of acute depression from which he was suffering when he arrived in Calais.

Having installed Cerissa together with innumerable pieces of hand-luggage in the cabin, he left her with Francine and walked round the deck.

He was a good sailor and the roughest sea had never perturbed him in the slightest. He found that as most of the passengers were feeling squeamish long before they left the Harbour, he had the deck almost to himself.

He was leaning over the rail, having a last glimpse of the coast of France receding into the distance, when Bobo came and stood beside him.

"*Pardon, Monsieur,* but there is a gentleman sitting on the other side of the ship who has drunk himself insensible."

"What about it?" Sheldon Harcourt asked.

"He has a wallet bulging with notes, *Monsieur.* If I do not take it, undoubtedly someone else will!"

"Do not be such a fool!" Sheldon Harcourt said sharply. "If you are caught you will be taken before the Magistrates and either hanged or transported!"

He thought Bobo looked startled, although it was always difficult to read the expression on his black face.

"The authorities are very strict about thieving in England," Sheldon Harcourt said. "For the sake of *Mademoiselle,* you must not be involved in anything shady which could bring us unwelcome attention. Do you understand?"

He spoke severely and Bob gave a little sigh.

"You are right, *Monsieur,* but it was easy pickings —very easy!"

39

"I will tell you when we are so desperate that we have to stoop to stealing," Sheldon Harcourt said. "Until then you will take no risks. That is an order!"

"I understand, *Monsieur*. I am at your service."

Bobo gave him a funny little bow and moved away, not without dignity.

Sheldon Harcourt turned back towards the sea.

He was well aware that his problems were only just beginning and somehow they were a challenge which he could not resist.

* * *

Planning his campaign with care, Sheldon Harcourt did not leave Dover on the day they arrived.

They all were tired and they found accommodation at the King's Head, which was in the same class as the Hôtel d'Angleterre, although the food was certainly inferior.

"I cannot eat this," Cerissa said the first night at dinner, wrinkling her nose over some tough mutton and watery vegetables.

"We will leave tomorrow," Sheldon Harcourt said consolingly. "As soon as I have managed to buy a Travelling Chaise."

"A Chaise?" Cerissa queried.

"Not only do I dislike the thought of rattling across country in a stage-coach," Sheldon Harcourt replied, "but it would certainly not be an impressive manner in which to arrive at Bath."

She was listening intently as he went on:

"The one thing we must try to avoid is for you to appear to be as penniless as the other émigrés living in England at the moment. If people think they may have to be responsible for your debts, they will very soon sheer off in the opposite direction!"

"We are to be rich?" Cerissa questioned with a little lilt in her voice.

"We have to pretend we are," Sheldon Harcourt answered, "which is a very different thing. For the rich are seldom generous except to themselves."

"That is true," Cerissa agreed. "My father so often

told me of the meanness amongst the Courtiers at Versailles. They would spend immense sums of money on their clothes, on diamond buckles, and jewelry for their wives, but they would make their servants wait months, sometimes years, for their wages."

"They also omitted to see the poor outside the gates and the hunger in Paris," Sheldon Harcourt said sharply. "They bought jewels while the people cried out for bread!"

"It is difficult to understand why they did nothing except enjoy themselves," Cerissa agreed.

Then with a change of mood she cried:

"Let us be rich and gay! Let us deceive the real rich and make them look stupid!"

"We will have to be careful," Sheldon Harcourt warned.

"*Oui, Monseigneur.* I will be very careful, and when I laugh they will not realise that I am laughing at them!"

"Let us be careful they do not laugh at us!"

"Oh, you are like Francine—you always look on the dark side! 'Be careful!' 'Do not do this!' 'Do not do that!' 'Do not take a risk!' 'Look before you leap!' I refuse to listen!"

She threw her arms up in a gesture of abandonment and looked so pretty as she did so that it was difficult to understand why Sheldon Harcourt said sharply:

"Behave yourself! Remember, you have only recently been bereaved. You are broken-hearted at the death of your father and mother, and having to flee from your own country."

"I may . . . not smile?" Cerissa asked in a small voice.

"Not often."

"I think I shall . . . return to France. I would rather be . . . guillotined than live in such . . . darkness . . . such misery. Not to smile! Do you want me to cry?"

"Not really. I loathe weeping women!"

"But if I do not smile . . . I cry! You have your choice. Perhaps you would like me to cry against your shoulder, *très pathétique*, very invitingly? Then you can comfort me."

"You can keep that scene for the man you marry," Sheldon Harcourt answered. "Now go to bed! I have a great many plans to make and you distract me."

"That is what Papa always said to Mama when he was composing a speech. Then he would kiss her and say that he did not mind being distracted."

There was a pause, then Cerissa said:

"Would you like to . . . kiss me . . . again?"

"Will you go to bed!" Sheldon Harcourt roared. "And call me *Monseigneur*. Do I have to speak to you about that again? Good-night!"

He held out his hand.

Cerissa dropped down in a low curtsey.

"*Bon soir, Monseigneur!*" she said in a meek voice.

Then as she rose she kissed the back of Sheldon Harcourt's hand.

* * *

They set off at noon the following day in a Travelling Chaise which Sheldon had purchased cheaply in Dover.

It was slightly old-fashioned but was well sprung and had belonged to a nobleman.

The panels were painted with a coat-of-arms and the wheels were bright yellow.

"How pretty!" Cerissa exclaimed when she saw it.

The two horses from the Posting-Inn were fresh and the best procurable, but Sheldon was already worrying over the expense.

When the Chaise was packed it was bursting with luggage and there was only just room for Francine and Bobo on the seat beside the driver.

Even then Bobo's feet rested on one of Cerissa's leather cases and Francine held on her lap a jewel-box embellished with a coronet.

The Heart Triumphant

As the sun was shining, Cerissa wore an attractive bonnet tied under her chin with satin ribbons.

But her sable-lined cloak was round her shoulders as there was a touch of frost in the winter wind which grew sharper as the day progressed.

"We will travel in easy stages," Sheldon Harcourt had said. "There is no point in arriving at Bath in a state of collapse and exhaustion."

"What you mean is that we shall need to keep our wits about us!"

"That about sums it up," Sheldon Harcourt agreed. "I am trying to remember if there is anyone I know who had a house in Bath or on the outskirts. But it is a very long time since I went there, in fact I think I was only seventeen at the time."

"Why did you go there then?" Cerissa asked.

"My mother had been ill and ordered by the Doctor to drink the waters. She also found that the cold in London and in Hertfordshire where we lived gave her a cough which seemed to linger on into the summer months."

"Was your mother very beautiful?"

"Very!" Sheldon Harcourt replied. "She died the year after we had been to Bath."

"Oh, I am sorry," Cerissa said. "You must have missed her."

"I did, and my father died two years later."

"So you were an orphan at almost the same age as I have become one!"

"That is something we have in common."

"There are a lot of . . . other things as . . . well," Cerissa insisted.

"What sort of things?"

She thought for a moment.

"I think we have the same taste, although we have not had much time to talk about it. Papa said that taste is very important, that when one person has good taste and another bad they are certain to fall out because they irritate each other."

43

"I think that is true," Sheldon Harcourt remarked, "although I have never thought about it before."

"I have no wish for you to be irritated by me, *Monseigneur*."

"Then behave as I wish you to do."

"I am trying," Cerissa said. "Do you not realise that I am trying? It is very disappointing if you do not appreciate my efforts."

Sheldon Harcourt smiled.

"I do appreciate them, but you do realise, Cerissa, that everything hinges on the impression we make when we arrive in Bath?"

He thought for a moment before he went on:

"We can be spectacular. We are so anyway, just by being ourselves, especially with Francine and Bobo in attendance. But, as you say, it must not be in bad taste, and our relationship must not in any way give rise to suspicion."

"I will be very young and very ingenuous," Cerissa promised, "and when you introduce me to gentlemen I will look at them wide-eyed and ask them to explain to me why the world is round!"

She gave a little laugh.

"I am sure men much prefer stupid women. It makes them feel superior."

"That is not the sort of remark you should make." Sheldon Harcourt corrected.

"But I am saying it only to you."

"Think it, but do not say it aloud," he admonished.

* * *

They spent the night in an attractive Inn where they were the only guests.

The Landlord welcomed them effusively and offered them the best bed-chambers after making the initial mistake of thinking they were husband and wife.

A fire was kindled in the private Parlour, and dinner, while somewhat dull and traditionally English, was at least, Cerissa conceded, edible.

She was tired and far less talkative than usual.

In fact, when dinner was over and Sheldon Harcourt sat in front of the warm fire with a glass of brandy in his hand he found his own head nodding.

He pulled himself to wakefulness and looked at the next chair to find that Cerissa was sound alseep.

She was curled up, her head on the soft cushion which Bobo had carried down for her before dinner, her gown covered with the white ermine rug.

Asleep with her face in repose she looked even younger and certainly more vulnerable than when she was talking and laughing animatedly and her eyes were sparkling.

Sheldon Harcourt sat looking at her for a long time.

It seemed to him incredible that when he least expected it he now found himself involved in this dramatic situation with a girl he had met only two days before but to whom he was now giving his whole-hearted attention.

Trustingly she had given her money into his keeping, but he had conscientiously paid all his own expenses out of his own funds.

He was hoping that as soon as he reached the gambling-tables he could augment his fortune as he had managed to do with considerable success all the time he had been in France.

He had the idea it would be easier to win in Bath than it had been in Paris.

"I shall make certain that I do not cost her a penny," Sheldon Harcourt told himself, looking at Cerissa, "and I have no intention of hanging round once I have found her a husband."

He wondered what sort of man would be prepared to marry an émigrée who had no reliable record of her antecedents and who was foisted on Society by a very dubious sort of Guardian.

Then he told himself that Cerissa was lovely enough to sweep aside criticism and certainly all caution.

Sheldon Harcourt's own life had been full of beautiful women.

Although he had been fastidious in availing himself of their charms, he knew cynically that if the gaming-tables failed him there would always be white arms to comfort him and generous fingers ready to fill his pockets.

And yet, amongst all the women he had loved and who had loved him, Sheldon Harcourt admitted that there had never been one at the same time as beautiful as Cerissa and as fascinating.

He thought any man on whom she set her heart would find it difficult to refuse the invitation in those large dark eyes, or the softness of those exquisitely curved lips.

He remembered how young and innocent he had found them that first night.

She had invited him to kiss her and he had done so, believing that if she was not the *Comtesse* de la Tour she was at least a woman of experience where men were concerned.

Then when he had felt her lips so weak and defenceless beneath his, he had known that half the things she had said at dinner were untrue.

What was more, the slender body he had held in his arms was that of a girl rather than a woman.

A less sophisticated man might have been deceived—but not Sheldon Harcourt!

As he watched Cerissa sleeping, he hoped with a fervency that surprised himself that she would find happiness in her life.

She was a child in so many ways and the world could be a rough, frightening place for children without someone to look after them.

Sheldon Harcourt found his head nodding again.

He rose to his feet, put out his hand to awaken Cerissa, then changed his mind.

She was lost in some secret dreamland from which it would be cruel to disturb her.

Instead he bent down and picked her up in his arms.

She stirred for a moment and turned her face confidingly against his shoulder.

As he carefully carried her up the oak staircase to her bed-chamber her hair smelt of a fresh sweet fragrance which made him think of spring flowers.

Francine was waiting for her.

There was a fire burning in the grate and the candles cast a golden glow on the low ceiling.

As Sheldon Harcourt entered carrying his burden the maid started to her feet.

"She is asleep," he murmured. "Try not to awaken her."

Very gently he laid Cerissa down on the bed.

Then as Francine hurried forward to attend to her sleeping mistress he went from the room, closing the door gently behind him.

Chapter Three

The days they were travelling seemed tedious in that the journey appeared at times to be interminable.

At the same time, there was always variety, always a new interest, not only for Cerissa, to whom everything was new and exciting, but also for Sheldon.

He found that there had been great changes in the five years that he had been away.

Roads, for one thing, were greatly improved, and the frost eliminated the soggy seas of mud in which he remembered the wheels often stuck and the horses found it hard to pull even a light vehicle, let alone a heavily laden one.

The first part of their journey was on the Dover road and as they turned west Sheldon was particularly interested in the mail-coaches.

In 1784, four years before he left England, he had met on several occasions John Palmer, the Member of Parliament for Bath.

Palmer had for some years been extremely dissatisfied with the state of the mails, as were a number of other people, but no-one had known what to do about it.

The long-distance delivery of letters and parcels was entrusted to men called "post-boys," who being secure as minor Civil Servants considered themselves to be above vulgar notions of speed or urgency.

"They lag behind the public stage-coaches, linger in Inns, and it has been averred with reason that they are in league with the road-thieves," Palmer declared on public platforms.

As well as being a politician he was a man of the theatre.

He ran playhouses in Bath and Bristol, and to produce the best talent he found it necessary to keep in touch with both actors and managers in London.

"My own private coach is more than twice as fast as the post-riders," he had told Sheldon, "and certainly more reliable."

John Palmer suggested to the Post-Master General that coaches like his own—light, compact, and capable of more speed than the more-roomy variety— should replace the rambling post-boys.

"It takes a post-boy something like fifty hours to reach Bristol from London," he said seethingly, "but my first coach completed it in fifteen."

Now Sheldon learnt that, since he had been away, a Palmer coach was delivering the mail from London to every major city in England.

"A postal revolution has taken place!" he told himself.

When the weather was fine he found it intolerable to be cooped up inside the Chaise and therefore made Francine ride inside with Cerissa while he sat on the box and more often than not tooled the horses.

The driver he had taken into his employment had been warmly recommended by the coach-builders in Dover.

Chapman was a man whom Sheldon had trusted on sight, and he knew from the way he handled his horses that he was fond of them as well as having great expertise as a driver.

The coachmen of England were in a class of their own, but those who handled the mail and also the stage-coaches had one concern only, to reach their destinations on time.

Before Sheldon left England he had often been appalled at the manner in which the horses were used.

In fact he often quoted the Spaniards, who said: "England is a Heaven for women and a Hell for horses!"

There was no doubt that to many coach-owners, horses were just nameless machines to be worked until they dropped and were then discarded into the knacker's-yard.

It was not the speed of the coaches which killed the horses so much as their weight. Excess loads of merchandise paid better than passengers.

And yet the English coachman, filled with porter, beef, and potatoes, his coloured handkerchief round his thick neck, a crimson and yellow waistcoat and swaggering jockey-boots, was one of the sights of England.

But the swaggering heroes of the coaching-yard were not the type of men whom Sheldon would take into his employment.

Chapman, whom he had engaged, was quiet and deferential. At the same time, he was not afraid to voice his opinion, and Sheldon liked him for it.

The fact that they were both outstanding drivers created a mutual respect between Master and servant and made the long journey pass more quickly than Sheldon had anticipated.

At the same time, the long hours of inactivity except for when he was driving gave Sheldon plenty of time in which to think about their financial position.

Although the purchase of their own Chaise had been expensive, he had learnt in Dover that one day in a hired Post-Chaise would cost four pounds eight shillings, with a chance that if there was a great demand and a shortage of animals he might be asked two pence a mile.

It would of course have been less expensive to travel by mail-coach, with the discomfort either of being crushed to death by the passengers inside or of freezing on the roof, which was cheaper.

There was also a risk of danger through drunken

drivers or vehicles breaking down in lonely parts of the countryside.

For Cerissa's sake, Sheldon was sure it was important that they should arrive in Bath appearing to be people of means, and not the impoverished adventurers they were in reality.

One consolation on the journey was that the Inns were comfortable and for the most part extremely efficient.

Bustling hosts and chamber-maids were ready to welcome them with steaming punch, mulled ale, and warming-pans. The beds were soft and the food, if nothing more, was at least edible.

Chapman not only knew the quickest and easiest route to Bath, he was also aware of which Inns were the best and those that should be avoided.

He failed only once to achieve the comfort that Sheldon paid for and expected.

It had been a day of dismal rain and sleet, which had forced the horses they had hired at the last Posting-Inn to proceed more slowly than Chapman had planned.

Finally, as it grew near to dark and there were patches of mist on the road, he told Sheldon that it would be unwise to proceed any further.

"I can see an Inn ahead, Sir. Shall we stop?"

"We had best do that," Sheldon agreed, "even if it proves uncomfortable. We might have an accident if we proceed once darkness has fallen."

"That's what I was thinking myself, Sir," Chapman said respectfully.

They drew up at the Inn, which was called the *Pig and Whistle* to find that it was old-fashioned and picturesque with beamed ceilings and large, open fire-places.

But the Inn-Keeper's wife was in the throes of child-birth, and the Inn-Keeper himself in too agitated a state to give them his attention except superficially.

It was then that Sheldon discovered how resourceful their own staff could be—Chapman, Francine, and Bobo took over the Inn.

Francine cooked, Bobo waited, and Chapman lit fires, filled warming-pans, and fetched the wine from the cellars.

"I would cook for you if Francine would let me," Cerissa said.

"You have had a long day," Sheldon answered, "and I forbid you to do any more."

"But . . . I would like to cook for you, *Monseigneur*," she said, "and actually I am a very good Chef. Papa was very particular about his food, and when we had inexperienced servants I always supervised the meals."

"That might come in useful sometime," Sheldon said, "but I think it unlikely."

"Papa always said it was important to be as knowledgeable as one's Chef, even if he did the hard work."

"That is true," Sheldon smiled, "but I have no intention of allowing you to do any donkey-work. You are a grand lady, remember, and you must behave like one."

He thought as he spoke that only a Lady of Quality would have behaved as Cerissa had during this journey.

She never complained, she never sulked or appeared to be out of temper, and usually she found something exciting to say about every stop they made.

She was thrilled by the countryside where the trees white with frost had a fairy-like beauty; by the small towns with their cobbled streets and black and white thatched houses; by the great open spaces where the moorland rolled away into an indeterminate distance, gaunt, barren, and oppressive under the winter sky.

Cerissa always seemed to be smiling, gay, and amusing.

If Sheldon had feared to find a spoilt, imperious

young woman who resented discomfort, he was certainly pleasantly relieved.

At the same time, everyone was glad when they reached the Fosse Way sweeping majestically over high ground northeastwards to Bath.

Sheldon remembered that it climbed the hills by Downside to Bath and that the road, which ran direct from Exeter to Lincoln, was one of the great legacies which the Romans had left behind them.

He had already told Cerissa that Bath had originally been a fashionable resort of the Romans because it was the only place in England where there were medicinal hot-springs.

"How fascinating!" she exclaimed.

Sheldon knew that the legend of how they had been discovered would amuse her.

"An Ancient British King," he related, "had a son called Bladard who suffered from leprosy. He wandered about the country, shunned by everyone, and became a swineherd."

Cerissa was listening entranced by the tale.

"Like Bladard," Sheldon went on, "the pigs had a skin disease. One day they came upon a steaming swamp near a river bank!"

"I know what happened!" Cerissa cried excitedly.

"The swine plunged in," Sheldon continued, "and wallowed in the hot mud. When at last Bladard managed to drive them out, their skins were healed."

"So Bladard tried it for himself also?" Cerissa suggested.

"Of course, and his leprosy vanished. Later the Romans built a city there which they named *Aquae Sulis*, the springs of Sul, a Celtic goddess."

"Can I bathe in them?" Cerissa enquired.

"I imagine so," Sheldon answered. "As I was only seventeen when I bathed in them myself, I was not particularly interested then in what arrangements were made for the female of the species."

"You were not interested in women at seventeen?" Cerissa asked in surprise.

53

Barbara Cartland

"Not particularly," Sheldon answered. "English boys develop later than their continental counterparts."

"Papa told me he was deeply in love when he was twelve!"

"Your father was a Frenchman!"

Cerissa supported her chin with her hand and looked at him reflectively.

"Perhaps you are cold and women find it difficult to arouse you to any ardency."

Sheldon glanced at her sharply, then realised she was teasing him.

"The love-life of your Guardian should not be of any interest to you!"

"It interests me very much! I am most curious."

"Then your curiosity will remain unassuaged," he said coldly.

Cerissa sighed in an exaggerated manner.

"I am compiling a list of the subjects about which I must not speak," she said. "Soon they will fill a book, and I shall publish them as '*Maximes pour les Jeunes Filles*,' written by a man who does not understand women."

Sheldon smiled, he could not help it.

He wondered how many of the beautiful ladies he had known in the past would agree that he did not understand them.

The trouble had always been that he understood them too well!

"I think you are trying to provoke me, Cerissa," he said. "If you continue, I may exercise my prerogative as a Guardian and give you a good spanking!"

She looked at him from under her eye-lashes to see if he was serious. Then she said softly:

"That would at least show that you are not entirely indifferent to me!"

"Do I appear to be indifferent?" Sheldon asked in surprise.

Cerissa sighed again.

"I am beginning to feel that I am just a commodi-

54

ty, a piece of merchandise which you are prepared
to sell to the highest bidder. You polish, varnish, and
paint me, you instruct, exhort, and admonish me; the
only thing that concerns you is how much money I
will make."

It was an unfair accusation and they both knew it,
but Sheldon played along with her fantasy by saying firmly:

"And of course if you are not salable, I can always dispose of you at a bargain price or perhaps dis-
pense with you altogether."

In answer Cerissa threw her cushion at him.

* * *

It was early in the afternoon when they reached
a desolate part of the countryside where there were
no cottages, no cattle grazing, and no pastures, but
an arid wasteland with here and there a group of
stunted trees or an isolated yew.

They might have been in Northern Spain rather
than Somerset, Sheldon thought, and it was difficult
to think that here on this forlorn, isolated moor they
were less than fifteen miles from the frivolities of
Bath.

It began to rain and he stopped the coach to join
her inside, leaving only Bobo to sit beside Chapman
for the last part of their journey.

He knew that a couple of miles further on there
would be a gentle down gradient towards what in the
distance was a blue mist coming from the Bristol
Channel.

As he climbed inside the Chaise, Francine would
have moved out, but he prevented her.

"It is beginning to rain, Francine," he said, "and it
is also extremely cold. We shall find more warmth in
the valley, but here there is no protection from the
wind."

"Are we nearly there?" Cerissa asked.

Wrapped in her fur-lined cloak and covered by
rugs, she looked like a small dormouse hibernating for
the winter.

But as Sheldon sat down beside her he thought that her voice still had a gay lilt in it, and her eyes were as bright as those of the small rodent of which she reminded him.

Francine sat opposite them with her back to the horses and they started off again at quite a good pace.

"It will not be long now," Sheldon said, "and may I congratulate you on being an exemplary traveller in every way?"

"I have not been a bore?" Cerissa asked.

"You are never that," Sheldon replied. "Unpredictable—yes, surprising at times, but I could present you with a diploma to put on record that you are never boring."

"Papa used to tell us what a nuisance his family were when he travelled with them. They were always wanting to stop the coach, they talked when he wished to sleep, or slept when he wished to talk. And *Madame la Duchesse* felt carriage-sick."

"I am sorry for anyone who suffers with that affliction."

"Papa said it was an affectation."

"I think your father was rather unfeeling."

"As you would be if I was continually whining, being sick, or wanting to stop when you wished to push on to our destination."

"You have done none of those things," he agreed, "and I suppose I should thank you."

"I would ... like you to do ... that."

Sheldon did not reply.

He was looking out the window, realising that they were leaving the empty moor behind and moving downhill, which made him think there might be a river at the bottom of the valley.

Then unexpectedly the brakes were applied and the carriage was drawn abruptly to a standstill.

"What has happened?" Sheldon exclaimed.

At that moment the door of the carriage was flung open and a masked man with a pistol in his hand put in his head.

Cerissa gave a little cry of terror and Francine too was startled into an exclamation of horror.

"'And over yer valuables!" the man said in a thick, uncultured voice.

There was no time to think, no time to move, except that Sheldon had his hand in the pocket of his great-coat and in that pocket was a loaded pistol.

No gentleman would have been so foolish as to travel without one, but because their journey had been so uneventful he had almost forgotten it was there until almost instinctively his finger was on the trigger.

He fired and the bullet went through the heavy cloth of his coat and entered the intruder's body just below the heart.

For a moment the thief seemed stunned both by the noise of the explosion and by the impact of the bullet.

Then as his mouth opened ludicrously and he fell backwards he fired the pistol he held in his right hand.

The bullet seared the top of Sheldon's arm, and the report and the smoke from the barrel seemed to fill the inside of the Chaise.

Outside, another man, who had pointed his pistol at Chapman and forced him to draw the horses to a standstill, turned his head at the second report.

He had been expecting one, but not two, and in that moment Bobo acted.

A long, thin dagger, sharp as a needle, shot through the air and caught the second highwayman in his throat.

As he fell backwards into the road, Chapman whipped up the horses and they were away.

It was Francine who managed to close the swinging door as they drove at break-neck speed down into the valley and up the hill on the other side of it.

Cerissa had thrust back her hood to attend to Sheldon.

"You are hurt, *Monseigneur!* You are hurt!"

Sheldon did not answer.

He was holding his left arm with his right and was aware that the blood had already seeped through from the layers of clothing to the outside of his great-coat.

"What shall we do? We must stop the bleeding!" Cerissa cried frantically.

"It is all right," he answered with difficulty. "It is not serious. He only winged me."

"It is serious," Cerissa insisted. "We must stop and I will bandage it for you."

"Let us get away first."

He was aware that Chapman was doing the best thing possible in taking them out of harm's way.

He suspected that there had been just the two men and he cursed himself for not having been more prepared in such an isolated spot.

It was to be expected that there would be thieves, footpads, and highwaymen in the vicinity of Bath, where the pickings from rich and important travellers would be better than anywhere else.

Too late he told himself that however inclement the weather he should have remained on the box of the Chaise until they reached a more inhabited part of the countryside.

Salisbury Plain and all the moors round Bath were noted for being dangerous to travellers, and he had forgotten it simply because he had been away from home for so long.

Francine had said nothing after her first exclamation of horror, but now she was bringing a number of handkerchiefs from her pockets and opening some of their light luggage to find others.

In one bag there was a linen hand-towel and producing a pair of scissors she began to cut it into long strips.

Still the Chaise hurried on and now Cerissa could see the crimson patch growing every second on the outside of Sheldon's great-coat.

"We must stop!" she said frantically even as

Chapman brought the horses to a standstill and Bobo jumped down from the box.

He pulled open the door.

"I killed him, *Monsieur!* My knife entered his throat at exactly the right spot!"

Bobo was obviously delighted with himself. Then he saw what had occurred inside and the grin vanished from his black face.

"*Monsieur* is injured!"

"*Monsieur* was shot by those villains," Francine answered.

Now that they were at a standstill, she was skilfully, with Cerissa's help, assisting Sheldon to take off his coat.

Bobo took a quick glance at his face and said:

"Cognac! That is what *Monsieur* needs—cognac!"

"Of course!" Cerissa agreed. "How stupid of me. Find his flask, Bobo. It is in one of the pockets."

Ministered to by both women and given brandy by Bobo, Sheldon found the waves of nausea which had followed the first shock of his wound receding rapidly.

By the time Francine had applied a pad and bandaged his arm skilfully, he was smiling and telling Cerissa not to fuss.

"You might have been killed!" she said in a low voice, and her large dark eyes were misty.

"I am quite certain he was an abominable shot!" Sheldon replied. "Most footpads are. They are all bluff and blister! But when it comes to the point they are usually ready to run away."

"I thought I should be so . . . safe in England," Cerissa said pathetically. "In France the . . . guillotine . . . but here . . . what do you call them . . . footpads?"

"Highwaymen ride horses, footpads thieve on their feet," Sheldon explained.

"I think these men had horses, *Monsieur*," Bobo interposed. "I saw two in the distance tied to a tree and thought nothing of it."

"I should have been sitting outside," Sheldon muttered. "Perhaps I had better do so for the rest of the journey."

"You will do nothing of the sort!" Cerissa cried. "Give Bobo your pistol, he will reload it and carry it himself. He is a good shot. Papa taught him so that he could protect Mama and me if we were alone in our little house. We were always afraid of robbers."

Sheldon did not seem inclined to argue and she drew the pistol from the pocket of his great-coat and handed it to Bobo.

"Now let us hurry on to Bath," she said. "The sooner we get there, the better! Then we can find a Doctor who will attend to *Monseigneur*."

They set off again and now it was difficult to make Sheldon comfortable.

They supported him with cushions, but even so, Cerissa, watching him anxiously, saw his lips tighten when the wheels passed over a rut or the horses jerked the Chaise.

The flask of brandy was nearly empty when after what had seemed like hours they began to rattle over the cobble-stones on the outskirts of Bath.

There was no time for Cerissa to stare out as she had intended to do at the fine buildings which Sheldon had described to her, or think of anything but that a Doctor must be procured and Sheldon got to bed.

Then as the carriage drew into the court-yard of the White Hart Hotel, where she knew they were staying, her practical common-sense and sense of the dramatic told her that she must turn this situation to her advantage.

Hastily she tidied what hair showed beneath the expensive fur of her cape and swiftly touched her lips from a pot of the red salve which she carried in her reticule.

A quick glance in the small mirror which she always had ready to hand told her that while she looked pale she also looked very pretty.

The Heart Triumphant

The Chaise drew to a standstill and liveried servants came hurrying down the steps to open the door.

But Bobo was there before them.

"Go in, Bobo. Announce that I have arrived and that there has been an accident," Cerissa said in French.

Obediently Bobo hurried up the steps to obey her command.

The White Hart, being the largest of the many Hotels which catered to the noble and important visitors to Bath, was also a place where it was fashionable to hold dinner-parties.

It was not very late, but Bath dined early and already the guests of Lord Walburton were congregating in the large open Hall.

The gentlemen were warming themselves in front of a large fire while they waited for their ladies, who had proceeded upstairs to set aside their wraps before entering the private Dining-Room which had been engaged by His Lordship for his guests.

Extremely elegant in their meticulously tied cravats and wearing white knee-breeches and silk stockings, the majority were not powdered, since the new fashion decreed that a gentleman's hair should remain as God made it.

It was a vogue which had aroused passionate resentment in the older generation, who asked what the world was coming to when a gentleman discarded his wig and powder and looked like a "cit" or a "pleb."

It was yet another way in which the Prince of Wales had rebelled against the formality of his father's Court.

It was in fact only at Buckingham Palace and Windsor Castle that the ladies still wore hoops and were obliged to be *en poudre*.

The conversation at the fireside inevitably concerned the announcement which had been made three days earlier that England had declared war on France.

"I am damned certain that we cannot afford a

61

war!" an elderly man remarked. "But in self-respect there was nothing else we could do."

"I am told that our ships are rotten and we have not enough sailors to man them," someone else remarked.

"The Army Command has been complaining for years that our weapons are out of date," a retired General roared. "But who would listen?"

"They will listen now," someone replied. "Not that I imagine a war with the Frenchies will last long! They have had some small success on the Continent, but the majority of their leaders are discredited."

"I am told that swine Talleyrand has arrived in London—a revoltingly profligate figure! I have told my wife that on no account are we to receive him."

"I should think not!" an ancient Peer agreed. "Why should we entertain these damned frogs, diplomats or not, whose only idea is to be at our throats in one way or another?"

This speech drew a murmur of applause from several other gentlemen, while they looked up to see their wives and daughters coming down the stairs towards them.

Attractively dressed in the full-skirted gowns which made them look as graceful as swans, their hair curled in the fashion which had been set by Mrs. Fitzherbert, every lady was glittering with jewels.

They had almost reached the bottom of the stairs when suddenly through the outer door of the Hotel there came running a strange little figure.

His black face, his claret livery with its gold buttons, the high cockaded hat he held in his hand, and his white gloves made him arrestingly noticeable.

He ran towards the Reception-desk which stood just at the bottom of the stairs, crying in a shrill voice which was clearly audible to everyone in the vicinity:

"*M'mselle la Comtesse* has arrived, but there has been an accident! The English *Milor* has been shot by footpads! A Doctor—we require a Doctor immediately!"

"Footpads?"

The word appeared to be repeated by everyone listening, and the Receptionist, a suave gentleman who welcomed every guest who arrived at the Hotel, exclaimed in horror:

"Do you mean that someone has been shot?"

"*Oui, oui, Monsieur*. Shot by footpads and dangerously wounded! *M'mselle la Comtesse* is distraught, as well she might be. A Doctor! Procure a Doctor!"

"It shall be done."

"And the gentleman! He must be carried to his room."

As Bobo finished speaking, Cerissa herself came through the doorway, looking exceedingly beautiful and at the same time agitated.

Without even a glance at the assembled company who seemed to have been immobilised, she addressed the Receptionist in her soft voice with its attractive accent:

"My servant will have told you, *Monsieur,* of the . . . terrible experience we suffered on our journey here."

"He has told us, Madam," the Receptionist replied. "I regret . . ."

"I am *la Comtesse* Cerissa de Valence," Cerissa interrupted, "and it is my Guardian, Mr. Sheldon Harcourt, who has been wounded. He was brave, very brave! We left two footpads dead beside the road. At least they will threaten no more travellers."

A tall gentleman with slightly greying hair who had been standing at the fireside came forward.

"I am deeply concerned, Ma'am," he said in a deep voice, "to hear of your misadventure. If there is any way in which we can be of assistance I am sure we will be only too glad to do so."

There was a murmur of approval to this speech.

Cerissa looked up at him, her eyes wide and frightened, her lips trembling, her long fingers interlocked as if they helped her to keep control of herself.

"It was . . . very frightening . . . *Monsieur*."

"I am sure it was."

"If you could . . . recommend a . . . Doctor."

As she spoke she glanced towards the door and through it the assembled company saw Sheldon Harcourt being carried in by four sturdy young servants.

He seemed to be very large, but even with closed eyes and a bandaged arm he managed to look elegant and extremely handsome.

Following him came Francine, the very picture of a respectful Abigail such as someone as young as Cerissa should have in attendance.

Almost as if they carried a corpse the servants proceeded up the stairs, the ladies who were descending drawing to one side to let them pass.

There were expressions of concern and sympathy on their faces as they looked at the prostrate man.

Cerissa wrung her hands.

"A Doctor . . . please . . . a Doctor!" she gasped. "My Guardian is the . . . only person in the world . . . I have left to . . . look after me. My father . . . the *Duc* de Valence . . . left me in his . . . charge even as he was taken to the . . . guillotine!"

There was a sob in her voice which moved every man in the room and the gentleman to whom she was speaking said hastily:

"My own Doctor is an excellent man! I will send for him immediately. There is no better Surgeon in the whole of Bath."

"*Merci, merci, Monsieur*," Cerissa said. "Will you tell me your name?"

"My name is Trevellyan—Sir Ralph Trevellyan."

"I am deeply grateful, Sir Ralph."

Cerissa swept him a curtsey. Then without a glance at anyone else she moved swiftly up the stairs after Sheldon and the servants, who were almost out of sight.

The Heart Triumphant

Only as she reached the first landing did she hear a babble of sound break out below as everyone talked at once.

In the large comfortable bed-room, which was one of the best in the White Hart, Sheldon was sipping another glass of brandy and looking very unlike the unconscious victim who had been carried up the stairs.

Only Cerissa and Bobo were in the bed-room while Francine was next door in the Sitting-Room checking the pile of luggage which had been brought from the Chaise by porters.

"We certainly made a spectacular entrance!" Sheldon remarked.

"We may even be thankful for the footpads!" Cerissa replied.

Then her tone changed as she said:

"Is it very painful? The Doctor should be here soon."

"It is not as bad as it was at first," Sheldon admitted.

"You looked most convincingly unconscious. You frightened even me!"

"If all else fails, I will get you a part at the Playhouse. I thought the bit about your father on the steps of the guillotine was very effective!"

"It is what we decided to say," Cerissa said defensively.

"What *you* decided," he answered, "but never mind, it will give them something to talk about, and that, after all, is what you wanted."

"Have you ever heard of Sir Ralph Trevellyan?"

"Never," Sheldon replied, "but I will find out about him from the Doctor. In the meantime, as Bobo wishes to put me to bed, you had best retire to another room."

"You would not like me to help?" Cerissa asked mischievously.

"You will do as you are told," Sheldon said briefly.

Because she knew there was nothing she could do which Bobo could not do better, Cerissa left him.

The Doctor was somewhat delayed, having been visiting a patient on the other side of Bath, and Sheldon was in fact running a temperature when he arrived.

The cleaning of the wound, although it was only a superficial one, left him shaken, even though he despised himself for not being impervious to pain.

He was in fact only too glad to take the laudanum which Dr. Price said would send him to sleep and take away the pain.

"Leave him to rest," the Doctor said to Cerissa when she received him in their private Sitting-Room, looking very young and pathetic in her black gown to which Francine had added skilful little touches of white.

Knowing how much Doctors liked to gossip, she lost no time in informing Dr. Price about herself.

She was quite certain that it would not be long before his distinguished patients were told about her father's execution and the sacking of their *Château* when so many historic treasures of the past had been looted or burnt.

"I feel for you very deeply, *Comtesse*," Dr. Price said, sipping a glass of excellent port which he had accepted with very little persuasion.

"Fortunately my father was wise enough to invest some money for me in England," Cerissa told him, knowing that this information would certainly be repeated, "and there are other émigrés in a much worse position than I am."

She smiled.

"I am especially fortunate to have a Guardian. Mr. Harcourt had always been a close friend of Papa, and luckily he was in France and could bring me to safety to your wonderful country."

"That was indeed fortunate," the Doctor agreed. "But I should have thought that Mr. Harcourt was

66

rather a young man to be saddled with the responsibility of a beautiful young woman?"

Cerissa's eyes gazed at him in all innocence.

"He *looks* young," she replied, "but really he is quite old. The same age, I think, as Papa. They have been friends for many years and I have always thought of *Monsieur* Harcourt as if he were my uncle."

"And why have you come to Bath?" Dr. Price enquired, taking another sip of his port.

"My Guardian knows that I often have a cough in the winter," Cerissa replied. "Besides, I could not face London at the moment, seeing that I am in deep mourning and could take little part in the entertainments."

She gave a deep sigh.

"Indeed . . . I would not . . . wish to do so."

"I can understand that," Dr. Price said briskly. "At the same time, we cannot have you moping. We must tempt you out, *Comtesse*. The Season is only just starting and it would be a pity for you to miss the many amusements which Bath can provide."

"You are very kind," Cerissa smiled, "but I feel as if I have left my youth behind me . . . in France."

She spoke so pathetically that the Doctor felt a constriction in his throat as he bade her farewell.

"I will call tomorrow and see my patient," he promised. "In the meantime, go to bed and try not to worry. You will dine upstairs, I suppose?"

"Of course," Cerissa said in a voice which told him that no other idea had even entered her mind, "and you must tell me how I may help my *pauvre, pauvre* Guardian. I should not wish to do anything until he is better."

"Then we must get him better quickly," Dr. Price said gallantly.

"I am so very . . . very grateful to you," Cerissa said in heart-felt tones.

She curtseyed to the Doctor in a manner which he found utterly entrancing.

As he hurried away full of information which he would lose no time in imparting to his other patients, Cerissa ran to Sheldon's room.

To her consternation, she found him in a drowsy state and incapable of listening to anything she had to tell him.

"There is no need to be perturbed, *M'mselle*," Bobo said. "He suffered much pain when the Doctor examined his arm, but the wound is clean. Give *Monsieur* a couple of days and he will be downstairs fit as a flea!"

Disconsolately, Cerissa went back to Francine in her own room.

"Bobo says *Monseigneur* will not be up for two days."

"Then the best thing you can do is to rest," Francine answered. "You are tired, as we all are, after that terrible journey."

"Only the last bit was terrible," Cerissa said. "I like being with *Monseigneur*. It is fun being alone with a man, Francine!"

"Then the sooner you find yourself a husband the better!" Francine snapped. "And from all I saw as we came in, there should be plenty to choose from one way or another."

"Englishmen are taller and better-looking than Frenchmen," Cerissa mused. "And at the same time they have a presence. They are authoritative. They believe the world lies at their feet for them to walk on."

Francine muttered something which Cerissa did not catch and she went on:

"It would be nice to belong to England, Francine. I want to be English and bear an English name."

"Well, hurry up and get yourself one," Francine said, "and it will be easier when you are looking pretty again."

"Again?" Cerissa asked quickly. "What is wrong with me now?"

"You're travel-stained and exhausted," Francine

68

replied. "What you need is forty-eight hours in bed! Then you'll be *très jolie, ma petite!*"

Cerissa gave a little yawn.

"It does sound rather alluring, and Bath can wait! At least I shall have *Monseigneur* to talk to, as we are *en suite*."

"He doesn't want to talk—that's for sure. So leave him alone!"

As she undressed, Cerissa thought that Francine must be tired too. It was unlike her to be so irritable. . . .

Chapter Four

The door opened and Cerissa put in her head.

She saw that Sheldon was awake and came into his bed-room, her eyes anxious as she looked at him.

"You are better?"

"Practically well."

He was sitting up in bed with his arm in a sling. He had been shaved, and his hair was arranged so that he looked his usual elegant self.

Cerissa ran towards him and he realised she was wearing a very attractive diaphanous négligée in pale blue gauze which accentuated the transparency of her skin and the darkness of her hair.

"It is so exciting, *Monseigneur!*" she said. "You are a hero! The newspapers are full of your bravery."

"The newspapers?" Sheldon asked sharply.

"Yes . . . they have written columns about you in the *Bath Herald* and have interviewed Chapman and Bobo about what occurred."

"Let me see."

There was a frown on his forehead which made Cerissa stare at him in a perplexed manner.

"You are not . . . pleased?"

"I have no wish to be in the newspapers," he said, "even if it is one which is published only in Bath."

He took the paper from her and saw that most of the front page was devoted to their exploits.

The headlines were dramatic:

The Heart Triumphant

The news was welcomed in Bath on Tuesday evening of the death of two notorious Highwaymen who had preyed on our visitors for over two years.

Known as "Black Joe" and "Red Rufus," the men intercepted coaches crossing the moorlands outside the City and robbed the travellers.

Their fierce appearance and bullying ways frightened the ladies into handing over their valuables and as they attacked only vehicles with no out-riders their pistols seldom evoked any argument.

But on Tuesday evening they met their match. Sheldon Harcourt Esquire, a gentleman of Fashion and a distinguished visitor to Bath, was accompanying his Ward, the Comtesse Cerissa de Valence, a daughter of the late Duc de Valence, when their coach was brought to a standstill.

From subsequent enquiries it appears that it was Black Joe who opened the coach door and pointed a pistol at the occupants, demanding their valuables. In the meantime, Red Rufus held the coachman and the Comtesse's black servant at gun-point.

Without replying to Black Joe's impertinent demands, Mr. Sheldon Harcourt shot the intruder through the heart and only as he fell did the Highwayman pull the trigger of his own pistol so that the bullet entered Mr. Harcourt's arm.

Red Rufus was taken off his guard. A dagger thrown exceedingly skilfully and with great force by the black servant embedded itself in his neck.

Both felons were found the following day dead on the moor with their horses tethered to a tree some distance away.

The Comtesse Cerissa de Valence and her Guardian are staying at the White Hart Hotel

and neither was available yesterday when a repre-
sentative of the newspaper enquired as to their
health.

Ted Chapman, however, their coachman, gave
evidence before the Magistrates.

We feel that the whole City of Bath is deeply
indebted to Sheldon Harcourt Esquire, for delivering us from these pests who have remained at
large for far too long.

"There!" Cerissa exclaimed as she saw that Sheldon had finished reading the report. "Is that not flattering?"

"It is the sort of publicity I do not wish to court,"
Sheldon replied coldly. "Let us hope it is of no interest
to the London newspapers."

Cerissa looked at him speculatively.

She realised that he was genuinely perturbed by
what he had read and shrewdly she guessed that there
were people in London who he was anxious should
not know of his arrival in England.

She was aware, however, that she would gain
nothing by asking questions and she therefore sat
down on the edge of the bed to say:

"I have so much to tell you. Francine would not
let me disturb you yesterday, and to be honest I slept
most of the day."

"So I learnt when I enquired," Sheldon remarked.

It was impossible for him to repress the admiration in his eyes when he looked at her.

The long rest had smoothed away the shadowy
lines of fatigue under her eyes.

Her dark hair as it fell over her shoulders nearly
to her waist had a buoyancy about it which seemed to
invite the rays of a pale sun shining through the window.

Outside, it was a cold but sunny day with a touch
of frost in the air which made everything seem to
sparkle with an enchanting brilliance. The lights of it

appeared to have been captured by Cerissa's eyes as she said excitedly:

"Such a lot of people have called on us. I have all their cards to show you and the Sitting-Room is filled with flowers."

Sheldon smiled.

"If we had planned it we could not have thought up a more dramatic way of making our appearance."

"That is true," Cerissa agreed. "One man who left his card told Francine that he was the Master of Ceremonies. What does that mean?"

"It means that you have the *entrée* into the Assembly Rooms, where you will meet all the most important people in Bath."

Sheldon's lips twisted a little cynically as he said:

"For the ordinary visitor it is expected that they should first make a formal call on the Master of Ceremonies so that their presence is recognised socially."

"But the Master of Ceremonies has come to us!"

"That shows how important we are," Sheldon replied mockingly, "and when you receive him you will of course pay our subscription."

"Do we have to pay?" Cerissa asked in surprise.

"I can assure you that even in Bath, as in life, one receives nothing for nothing!" Sheldon said cynically.

He saw the expression on Cerissa's face and added:

"Never mind about that. You have your foot on the social ladder, my dear, and that is what you want."

"You do not sound very pleased about it."

"But of course I am pleased for your sake."

"It will only be exciting if you . . . enjoy it too."

"What you are going to do," Sheldon said, "is to dress yourself, then go with Francine to the Pump-Room. I think you will find that everyone is waiting for you to make an appearance.

"In the . . . Pump-Room?" Cerissa asked.

"You will take the waters. They are incredibly nasty, but remember the ostensible reason for which we have come to Bath is your health. Force yourself at least to swallow a drop or two."

"And then . . . ?"

"What happens after that you must play by ear," Sheldon said. "The Doctor does not wish me to get up until tomorrow."

"Oh, no! That is too disappointing!" Cerissa protested. "I was hoping and longing for us to do everything . . . together."

"Perhaps it is better the way it is," Sheldon remarked. "You will look pathetic in your black, and I am certain there will be a great number of gentlemen ready to console you for your unfortunate experience with the footpads and for the absence of your Guardian!"

He spoke so sarcastically that Cerissa looked at him uncertainly. Then he said crossly:

"Hurry, hurry! And get out of that indecent garment and into something more respectable. Even a Guardian should not be tantalised by a young woman *en déshabillé*."

Cerissa rose from the bed.

"You do not like this négligée? It is my best and I thought it very pretty."

"It is too damned pretty for you to be seen in it," Sheldon replied. "Now, get out of my room and let me behave as the invalid I am supposed to be!"

"Men are always cross when they are ill," Cerissa said, "but because I want you to get well quickly I will do exactly as you tell me. You should be pleased about that if nothing else!"

"Hurry up and get dressed," Sheldon ordered.

As she went from the room he picked up the *Bath Herald*.

* * *

It was late by Bath standards when Cerissa, escorted by Francine, entered the Pump-Room.

With its Grecian colonnades it was an extremely fine building and had been partially finished by Thomas Baldwin, who was still working on the outside.

Cerissa could not fail to be impressed by the splendid room with its great columns, a curved recess at each end, and its Musicians' Gallery.

In a niche stood a statue of a plump gentleman who she was afterwards to learn was Beau Nash, the creator of fashionable Bath at the beginning of the century. He had in fact made it England's finest Spa.

She was, however, on this, her first visit, concerned with making her way to where she could see a woman elegantly attired in a high, full, be-ribboned muslin cap, handing out glasses of the celebrated medicinal water.

Cerissa walked slowly and with dignity, her eyes lowered modestly as she pretended not to be aware that she was the cynosure of all eyes.

There was not such a crowd as there had been earlier in the morning when the Pump-Room was filled with invalids.

Now those drinking the waters had gathered to meet their friends, to see and be seen. They were in fact passing the morning in a congenial fashion before they dispersed towards the Library, the Reading-Rooms, and the Coffee-Houses.

Cerissa had only walked halfway down the room when a man moved to her side and she looked up to recognize Sir Ralph Trevellyan.

He appeared to be even better-looking and more impressive than he had on the night of her arrival. As he bowed he said:

"It is with great pleasure, *Comtesse,* that I see you are better. I called yesterday to hear you were receiving no visitors and I was afraid that you were suffering from your horrific experience the previous day."

"*Bon jour,* Sir Ralph," Cerissa answered, curtseying to him very prettily. "It was extremely kind of you to call and even kinder to leave me that magnificent bouquet of flowers. *Merci mille fois!*"

"It was a very small tribute, considering how much this town owes you and your gallant Guardian."

"*Vous êtes bien amiable,*" Cerissa said, "but it was an experience which I hope never to repeat."

"I can understand that."

"We are fortunate," Cerissa said in a brave voice, "that it was no . . . worse."

"Dr. Price tells me that Mr. Harcourt is not too badly wounded."

"Dr. Price is *très sévère,*" Cerissa said with a smile. "He will not allow *Monseigneur* to rise, although he wishes to do so."

"Quite right!" Sir Ralph exclaimed. "But in his place please allow me the honour of looking after you."

"I hope I am . . . safe," Cerissa said in a nervous tone. "And I have my maid with me."

"There are no further dangers of that sort, I assure you," Sir Ralph replied. "But will you understand when I tell you that everyone in Bath is anxious to make your acquaintance?"

"To meet . . . me?" Cerissa asked in assumed surprise.

"Yes, indeed. You are not only the heroine of a dramatic incident, you are also, if you will pardon me for saying so—very beautiful!"

Cerissa managed to look adorably confused, and while she was apparently at a loss for words Sir Ralph introduced her to various ladies.

She found it difficult to hear their names but was in fact aware that they all had titles.

Cerissa noted they were not half as smartly dressed as she might have expected. She was however aware that their satin, velvet, and silk gowns were of extremely expensive materials and the jewels they wore were of the finest quality.

She realised shrewdly that there was no need for ladies of high distinction to be ostentatious or even ultra-fashionable. Their position in Society did not depend on personal adornment.

She guessed correctly that her modest appearance without jewels and wearing black created an excellent impression.

Also she had a dignity of pride and bearing without appearing too self-assured.

Cerissa deliberately did not remain chatting for long with Sir Ralph's friends.

Instead, she said that Dr. Price had insisted that she should take the waters.

They moved towards the counter where Sir Ralph procured a glass for her.

Cerissa had one sip and recognised the truth of Sheldon's warning when he told her she would not like it.

The taste was in fact, she thought, quite revolting, but she was too tactful to say so, as holding her glass in her hand she made no effort to drink from it again.

"Let me show you the King's Bath," Sir Ralph suggested.

"You mean we can see the hot baths from here?" Cerissa enquired.

"Yes, indeed. The King's Bath is right under the Pump-Room windows," Sir Ralph told her.

He led her to the window and she looked out to see a number of people who she realised were patients up to their necks in the steaming water.

To Cerissa's surprise, both men and women bathed together.

The ladies were wearing jackets and petticoats of brown linen with chipped hats, some of them with cherry or blue ribbons.

"How extraordinary!" she exclaimed.

Sir Ralph laughed.

"It certainly appears to be a little strange the first time one sees the Bath, but people will do any-

thing to be cured of their ailments, and there is no
doubt that this city is extremely proficient at doing
that."

"But I should hate to bathe together with all
those people!" Cerissa protested.

"It is slightly undignified," Sir Ralph agreed.

"What happens to their clothes when they leave
the water?"

"They are stripped by old women," Sir Ralph
answered, "and wrapped in blankets; then most of
them are taken back to their lodgings in Bath-chairs."

Cerissa laughed.

"What is a Bath-chair?"

"You will soon find out," Sir Ralph answered. "I
think they must have been invented in Nash's day,
and are very much in vogue for the transport of invalids. Look, there is one!"

He pointed to a chair with large wheels which
was being pushed along the Pump-Room floor by a
servant.

In it sat a very old, fat woman, bedecked in
diamonds, with her hands in a fur muff.

Cerissa laughed, she could not help it.

"It will be a long time before you have to travel
in one," Sir Ralph said reassuringly. "Many people
find the sedan-chair, which in this town is also called
a Bath-chair, useful for when they go out to dinner. If
it is only a short distance, it saves bringing out their
horses."

"I have travelled in a sedan-chair before now,"
Cerissa said, "but it seems so funny to call it a Bath-
chair."

"Everything in Bath is an advertisement for the
city," Sir Ralph explained. "There is also a biscuit
called a 'Bath Oliver,' which was invented by a
famous physician, Sir William Oliver."

"I hope it is more palatable than the water!"
Cerissa exclaimed.

Sir Ralph took the glass from her hand.

"Do not try to drink any more. I will not give you away to Dr. Price!"

"Thank you," Cerissa smiled, "and I think I should return now to my Guardian. He will wonder why I am away so long."

"There is so much more I want to show you and so many people who I know wish to meet you."

"Perhaps another time," Cerissa said vaguely.

"May I take you driving this afternoon?" Sir Ralph enquired. "It is a lovely day and I should like to show you the beauties of the city."

Cerissa hesitated and he said insistently:

"Please come with me. It would give me more pleasure than I can possibly express."

"I think perhaps I had better ask my Guardian," Cerissa said. "I am new to England, and I would not wish to do anything which is not correct. In fact I am sure he would be very angry with me if I did!"

"He is strict with you?"

"Very strict," Cerissa replied a little sadly. "He tries to take the . . . place of my . . . father."

She gave a little sigh and Sir Ralph said hastily:

"I know how lonely and unhappy you must feel, but we will try in England to make you forget your sufferings in France."

"It would be impossible for me to forget," Cerissa said in a low voice, "but perhaps with time it will not seem quite so . . . agonising."

"You are very brave."

"I . . . try to be, but I am . . . not always . . . successful."

"If you ever need a friend," he said in a low voice, "I am always there, ready to serve you."

She gave him a quick glance, then looked away as if she was embarrassed.

"I think I . . . should go . . . back to the . . . Hotel."

"I will escort you there," Sir Ralph said firmly.

They walked back with Francine only a foot or so behind them.

As it happened, the White Hart was very near to the Pump-Room and the journey was completed in a few minutes.

"I can see that Bath is very beautiful," Cerissa said, looking round her.

"I will show you all the new Squares and Crescents of which the people of Bath are so proud," Sir Ralph said. "We can drive in my Phaeton!"

"I cannot promise to come with you until I have discussed it with *Monseigneur.*"

"Would it be possible for you to ask him now?" Sir Ralph enquired. "And perhaps your maid could bring me the answer?"

"I will do that," Cerissa agreed, "if he is not asleep."

"Then I will wait here," Sir Ralph said as they reached the Hall of the Hotel.

"Thank you for being so kind to me," she said in a child-like voice.

Then she left him to walk slowly up the broad staircase, well aware that he was watching her as she went.

She knocked on Sheldon's door and burst in at the same time.

"I have been such a success!" she exclaimed. "Sir Ralph Trevellyan, the man who sent us Dr. Price, is at my feet!"

She crossed the room as she spoke to sit down on the side of Sheldon's bed.

"He wishes to take me driving this afternoon in his Phaeton," she continued. "I said I could not possibly accept without your permission, and that you were very strict with me!"

"From all I gather from the Doctor," Sheldon said after a moment, "Sir Ralph Trevellyan is a very rich man—extremely wealthy. But this is the first time he has been to Bath and the Doctor knows nothing else about him."

"What else is there of importance?" Cerissa asked.

"Shall I go driving with him, or shall I keep him in suspense for another day?"

"He may have—other interests," Sheldon remarked sourly.

"He does not appear to have," Cerissa answered. "All the ladies he introduced me to in the Pump-Room were middle-aged or elderly, and, I am quite certain, had husbands and half-a-dozen children somewhere at home!"

"The Doctor says Trevellyan is here alone and has taken a suite at York House, which I understand is a more exclusive Hotel than this."

"Should we have gone there?" Cerissa enquired.

"Perhaps. But as it happens I think this has turned out for the best. The Doctor tells me that all Bath is talking of our appearance, when the guests were assembling for Lord Walburton's dinner-party."

"I am lucky . . . so very lucky!" Cerissa cried. "Ever since I reached Calais everything has been like a wonderful dream. I am keeping my fingers crossed just in case you disappear."

"I thought we were talking about Sir Ralph Trevellyan?"

"He is interested in me, and, as you know, I need to meet a number of rich *Beaux* before I make my choice," Cerissa replied. "But you are different. Without . . . you none of this could have . . . happened."

There was a note of sincerity in her voice which was unmistakable.

"Thank you," Sheldon said dryly, "but as time is not on our side I suggest you go ahead with your charade as quickly as possible."

There was a pause.

"You are thinking of . . . money?" Cerissa asked.

"That is certainly one of the things which worries me."

"And the others?"

"There is no need to burden you with them at the moment. Accept Sir Ralph's invitation and see what

you can find out about him. There is no point in
wasting your charms."

"No . . . of course not," Cerissa agreed.

As she rose from the bed to find Francine, the
excitement seemed to have gone from her eyes and
she moved slowly.

* * *

The drive with Sir Ralph was successful.

Cerissa was able to admire without reservation
first his up-to-date and expensive Phaeton, drawn by
a pair of magnificent horses, and secondly Bath itself.

There was no doubt that Queen's Square, the Cir-
cus, and the Parade were exceptionally fine examples
of architectural planning.

"I am only hoping that war with France will not
prevent from being put into execution all the plans
that have been made for the beauty of Bath," Sir
Ralph said.

"Surely the war will not last long?" Cerissa asked.

"I certainly hope not," he replied, "but there is
always the possibility that a war on the Continent
could drag on almost interminably."

Cerissa gave a little sigh.

"There is enough suffering in France already."

"I can understand you feeling that. Let us talk of
something more pleasant—yourself, for example."

"I think you know all about me already," Cerissa
replied, "and I cannot for the moment bear to talk
of happier times before the . . . Revolution."

There was a little tremor in her voice before she
continued:

"And so, Sir Ralph, let us talk about you. Tell
me about yourself."

"I live in a very large house," he answered. "It is
in Oxfordshire."

"And you live alone?"

"Except when I have my friends to stay, which is
very frequently."

"I can understand that you need them, otherwise you might feel lonely."

"That is true," Sir Ralph agreed, "and I think you would find my house not only beautiful but also comfortable. Perhaps when you leave Bath you and your Guardian will visit me there?"

"Could we really?" Cerissa asked. "Oh, I would love that! I have heard so much about the great country houses of England, and I would love to stay in one!"

"I expect your Guardian has been talking to you of his own family mansion," Sir Ralph said. "Donnington Hall is certainly extremely impressive—overwhelmingly so."

Cerissa was silent.

She could not admit that she had never heard of Donnington Hall or that Sheldon was in any way connected with it.

"Tell me more about your house," she suggested.

Sir Ralph was quite willing to speak of the treasures which his ancestors had accumulated over the years, of his Park, laid out by Capability Brown, and the Palladian front, which had been erected by his father.

Sir Ralph did not keep Cerissa out long because as soon as the sun lost its warmth it began to grow very cold.

"There will be a black frost tonight," he predicted as he turned his horses toward the White Hart. "At the same time, we are warmer in Bath at this time of the year than in any other city in England."

"Then I feel that I am fortunate to be here," Cerissa smiled.

"And we are fortunate to have you," Sir Ralph said gallantly.

He was drawing up to the front of the Hotel as he said:

"I wonder if your Guardian would permit me to take you to dine this evening with Lady Imogen Kenridge."

Cerissa looked at him enquiringly and he explained:

"Lady Imogen is a sister of the Marquess of Wychwood. She is here with her mother, the Dowager Marchioness, but as she is a widow she has a separate establishment."

Sir Ralph drew his horses to a standstill as he went on to explain:

"Lady Imogen has a delightful house in Queen's Square. I know she would be delighted if you would be her guest. She actually saw you when you arrived as she was dining with Lord Walburton."

"I would love to accept," Cerissa replied, "but I must of course first ask my Guardian."

"I will send one of my servants to await your reply in half-an-hour's time."

He smiled as he added:

"It may sound a little informal to invite you so casually, but I know that Lady Imogen will write to you a personal note as soon as I inform her that you are free."

"Thank you for a most interesting and delightful drive," Cerissa said.

Sir Ralph threw his reins to the groom and jumped down from the Phaeton to assist her to the ground.

He held her hand a little longer than was necessary. Then as she moved up the steps of the Hotel he said insistently:

"Please—come this evening. I shall be so disappointed if you refuse."

There was something boyish in his request and Cerissa was smiling as once again she walked up the stairs to Sheldon's room.

Her cheeks were glowing from the cold and she looked very lovely as she entered the warm bedchamber with its brightly burning fire.

"He is certainly intrigued with me!" Cerissa said without preamble. "He has asked if he can take me this evening to dine with a Lady Imogen Kenridge."

"Who?"

"Lady Imogen Kenridge. I am sure I have the name right. The daughter of the Marquess of Wychwood. Her father must be dead, since Sir Ralph said her brother is now the Marquess."

"Yes, that is right."

"She is a friend of yours?"

"No, not a friend, but I know about her."

There was something in his tone which made Cerissa look at him sharply.

"You do not wish to see her again?"

"No, it is nothing like that, but she might know of my past, and I was hoping to avoid that."

"Sir Ralph said that your family house was called Donnington Park."

"So they do know," Sheldon said almost beneath his breath. "I suppose it was impossible to keep it a secret unless I travelled under another name."

"Keep what a secret?" Cerissa enquired.

"I will tell you about it sometime," he answered, "but for the moment I imagine that your importunate *Beau* is waiting to hear whether you can dine with him tonight."

"With Lady Imogen, not just him alone," Cerissa corrected.

"I should hope not!"

There was a pause, then he said irritably:

"Well, what are you waiting for? Tell him you are only too glad to agree and are ready to jump into his arms as soon as he holds them out. That is what you want, is it not?"

The roughness of his voice brought a look of uncertainty to Cerissa's eyes.

"I thought it was what we . . . both wanted," she replied. "He is a very . . . rich man, and he lives . . . alone."

"You are ready to marry him?"

There was silence for a moment before Cerissa said hesitatingly:

"I am . . . not quite . . . sure about that . . . but at

least he moves in the right . . . circles. He knows the right people . . . those I want to know."

"Then write your note," Sheldon snapped. "Tell him that you are waiting eagerly with palpitating heart for him to collect you, as I assume he is going to do."

Cerissa walked across the room.

"I think what you need," she said, "is a glass of the medicinal water from the Pump-Room. After that, anything will seem pleasant!"

She went from the room and Sheldon threw himself back against his pillows, feeling rather ashamed of himself.

'The sooner I stop behaving like a spoilt child,' he thought, 'the better! I shall not feel so irritable once I am up.'

Then he told himself that perhaps his enforced inactivity was all for the best.

He rather doubted whether the invitation would have been issued so promptly if it had had to include himself also.

There was nothing that appealed more to a man's gallantry than a courageous young woman fighting her way alone in a difficult world. And obviously Cerissa was exploiting the situation very much to her advantage.

He, however, had an idea about the evening, and sent for Francine. When she came, he said abruptly:

"You will accompany *Mademoiselle* when she goes out to dinner. Travel with her in the carriage and wait at the house, so as to return with her."

Francine looked surprised and Sheldon explained:

"We must safeguard *Mademoiselle*'s reputation. It would be a mistake for her to appear over-eager."

"*Monsieur* is very wise."

There was approval in Francine's voice and in her eyes.

"I well know the Social World and its poisonous tongue," Sheldon remarked as if to himself.

He did not see Cerissa again until she came into his room dressed for dinner, to ask his approval of her appearance.

She did in fact look lovelier than he had ever before seen her, in a gown of black gauze which had belonged to her mother. Her bare shoulders were almost startlingly white against the softness of the material.

The gown revealed Cerissa's exquisite figure and encircling her neck were her mother's pearls.

Francine had arranged her hair so that it looked as if its curls and waves were entirely natural and the only touch of colour was supplied by two small white rose-buds caught in the dark tresses.

Cerissa's large eyes seemed almost to fill her heart-shaped face, and as she stood at the foot of the bed, inviting Sheldon's inspection, he knew it would be hard for any young woman to look more lovely.

He felt she was really unique, quite different from any other young girl he had ever seen before. He was certain that she would captivate all the male guests at tonight's dinner, even if the women resented her.

"*Voila!* Do I look as you would wish me to do?" Cerissa asked, as he did not speak.

"I am sure you do not wish me to add my plaudits to those of the crowd?" Sheldon replied sourly.

"Are you still cross?" Cerissa enquired.

He did not answer and she went to the bed-side to take his hand in hers.

"If I did what I would prefer to do, I would stay here with you," she said in a low voice. "We could have dinner together and we could talk about all the things I want to know and which only you can teach me."

Her fingers tightened on his as she went on:

"But I know that you are worrying about money, and just only to eat is expensive."

"You are quite right," Sheldon interposed. "Forgive me for being like a bear with a sore head, but I resent being ill."

"Of course you do. All men do," Cerissa said wisely.

"Go and enjoy yourself and do not worry about your appearance. You will bowl them over!"

Cerissa looked at him enquiringly.

"Bowl . . . what does that mean?"

He smiled.

"It means you will leave them gasping—be a *succès fou*—and undoubtedly the toast of Bath!"

He saw the light in her eyes and laughed.

"You are very beautiful! That is what you want me to say, is it not? Well, I have said it. Now go."

Cerissa bent forward.

"*Bon soir, Monseigneur,*" she said, and kissed his cheek.

* * *

The house in Queen's Square was, as Cerissa realised on entering the front door, most impressive.

There were a large number of servants wearing blue livery with silver-crested buttons.

As Sir Ralph escorted her up the carved staircase she heard the chatter of voices and realised that the dinner-party was larger than she had expected.

There were in fact about thirty people present in the Salon with its five crystal chandeliers and draped curtains of blue brocade.

The walls were white, picked out with gold, and as soon as Cerissa saw her hostess she realised that the colours, like the house itself, were a fitting background for its owner.

Lady Imogen at twenty-five was at the height of her beauty, and Cerissa, who had been expecting someone much older, experienced a shock.

Having been told that Lady Imogen was a widow, she had supposed she would be about the age of Sir Ralph. The young goddess, in pink, white and gold, took her breath away!

Lady Imogen had in fact been proclaimed an "Incomparable" from the moment she left the School-Room.

At seventeen she had taken London by storm, at eighteen she had married Julian Kenridge, son and heir of an immensely wealthy Peer, whose wild behaviour and eccentric ideas were the talk of the *Beau Monde*.

He had killed himself three years later riding blind-folded in a ridiculous midnight steeple-chase, for a wager of five hundred guineas.

It was a senseless way for him to lose his life but Julian Kenridge had never had any sense except perhaps in his choice of a wife.

Lady Imogen had not mourned him excessively; she had merely found it delightful to be a widow at twenty-one with a large fortune and practically every man in London seeking her favours.

Her family had been anxious to marry her off again as quickly as possible, but she had refused every offer and insisted on remaining her own mistress and, thanks to her husband's wealth, beholden to no-one.

Her amatory exploits were the talk of St. James's. But with her beauty and wealth and rank as a Marquess's daughter it was impossible for anyone to ostracise her. And Lady Imogen invariably got her own way.

She had seen the spectacular arrival of Cerissa and Sheldon, and it had amused her simply because it was unusual.

She found Bath a bore, and yet it was convenient to leave London occasionally. Her mother's ill health had this year provided an excellent excuse for running away from a love-affair which was getting out of hand.

Despite the number of her ardent admirers who followed her to the Spa, after a month of the petty regulations originally imposed by Beau Nash, Imogen found that she was growing bored.

She looked round for something to titillate her

fancy and found it when she saw Sheldon Harcourt being carried upstairs.

One glance at the recumbent figure and handsome face had told her that this was what she had been waiting for.

Lady Imogen was used to giving way to her impulses however extravagant. Once she had set her sights on an objective, she never allowed anything to divert her from her goal until she got what she wanted.

She made up her mind before she entered the Dining-Room that evening that Sheldon Harcourt would mean something in her life. It was only a question of how quickly she could meet him.

She had seen Sir Ralph talking to Cerissa at the Pump-Room that morning and after that the way was clear.

"I am so delighted to meet you, *Comtesse,*" she said as Sir Ralph introduced Cerissa. "I know how distressing it must be for you to arrive alone in a strange town."

"My Guardian is with me," Cerissa said in a soft voice.

"But, alas, he is *hors de combat,*" Lady Imogen said, "and so we must try to look after you until he is well enough to do so."

"Your Ladyship is very kind," Cerissa murmured.

"That is what everyone wants to be where you are concerned," Lady Imogen said. "Let me introduce you to my friends."

She took Cerissa round the room and in the English fashion gabbled the names so quickly that it was impossible for her to remember them.

But she told herself that Sir Ralph could tell her afterwards who was of importance, and she soon realised that all the younger men in the party were obviously attached to her hostess.

She was relieved to find that at dinner she was seated beside Sir Ralph. He was able to tell her who most of the other guests were and some amusing things about them.

Cerissa found herself laughing a little unkindly at an elderly Peer whose third wife was spending his money so quickly that he had brought her to Bath for a change of scene—only to find that she dominated the gaming-tables and was in fact losing more than she had done in London.

One of the younger men, a Mr. D'Arcy Arbuthnot, had been trying to marry an heiress for years, but the girl who had kept him dangling all last year had done so deliberately to teach him a lesson.

When he actually proposed, he was given a sharp set-down.

There were several men who looked very presentable but who were already married.

There were others who were so decrepit that despite their high-sounding titles and large bank-balances Cerissa knew with a little shudder that she could never even consider marrying them.

What it came down to, she told herself at the end of the dinner, was that Sir Ralph was the only eligible gentleman present.

It was with a feeling of relief that she realised that despite her hostess's unparalleled beauty he was still looking at her in the same admiring manner as he had during the afternoon.

After dinner they had all played card-games of some sort, and Sir Ralph had insisted on being Cerissa's Banker.

"Perhaps it is wrong of me to let you do so," she had said tentatively, wide-eyed.

"I am honoured to be in such a position," he answered, "and I am sure that, as a refugee from France, you cannot afford to throw money away on anything as nonsensical as a game of chance."

"I am not penniless like so many other poor émigrés," Cerissa said in a child-like voice, "but I do not yet know how much money Papa had invested in

91

England. I know there is some, but of course the bulk of his great fortune was in France."

"I am sure of one thing," Sir Ralph said. "Wherever you may be, wherever you may go, Comtesse, your face will always be your fortune."

"Thank you," Cerissa smiled.

She was not fortunate with the cards and Sir Ralph paid her debts.

When they came to go, Lady Imogen pressed her hand most warmly.

"I have not had a chance to talk to you, which is disappointing," she said. "I love France, I love the French people, their Art, and their civilised way of looking at life. We must be great friends, you and I, *Comtesse*."

"Thank you," Cerissa replied.

"Now, when can we meet again?" Lady Imogen asked.

She thought for a moment, before she exclaimed:

"Why not tomorrow? And I must meet your Guardian. Could you both come to luncheon?"

Cerissa hesitated.

"Dr. Price has said that *Monseigneur* may get up tomorrow, but whether he would be allowed to go out . . ."

"I think it would be good for him," Lady Imogen interrupted. "I tell you what I will do: I will send my mother's carriage, which is built especially for invalids, to the Hotel to convey you both here!"

She smiled as she continued:

"We will not have a party. That I am sure would be too much for your Guardian. There will be just ourselves, and of course dear Sir Ralph. Then as soon as Mr. Harcourt feels in the least tired I will send you back."

She looked at Sir Ralph.

"Is that not a good idea?"

"Very good from my point of view!" he agreed.

"Then that is settled," Lady Imogen said before Cerissa could speak. "Unless I hear from you, *Com-*

tesse, the carriage will be outside the White Hart Hotel tomorrow at noon."

"You are very kind," Cerissa replied.

There was nothing else she could say.

Only as she stepped into Sir Ralph's carriage, followed respectfully by Francine, did she feel instinctively that she was being manoeuvred, although how and for what reason she was not certain.

Anyway, she told herself, Sheldon would be interested in the house, the pictures, and of course Lady Imogen.

Then as she sat beside Sir Ralph driving back towards the Hotel she thought with a sudden and uncomfortable disquiet that he might be too interested.

Lady Imogen was very beautiful!

Chapter Five

"There are so many things we can do in Bath," Lady Imogen said gently, "but it has been very dull for me until—now."

There was no mistaking the accent which she put on the last word or the fact that her blue eyes looked into Sheldon's face with an undisguised invitation in them.

He was well aware from the moment he arrived at Queen's Square that Lady Imogen's interest lay not in Cerissa but in himself.

He was too experienced not to be alert to Lady Imogen's intentions, and as the luncheon progressed the cynical twist to his lips became more pronounced, as did the mocking expression in his eyes.

He had debated with himself whether it was wise to accept on Cerissa's behalf another invitation from her hostess of the night before.

He thought in fact it might be more advantageous for her to appear in the Assembly Rooms, where the social figures gathered, and have a variety of choice before she became in everyone's mind too closely involved with Sir Ralph Trevellyan.

Then he decided that there could be no social circle higher than that enjoyed by Lady Imogen and her mother, the Dowager Marchioness, and that at the party the night before there had been many guests of importance.

Sheldon was well aware that the number of

young men who would come to Bath was strictly limited.

The Spa really catered to the elderly and the sick, and it was only Beau Nash who had been clever enough to make it a recognised rendezvous for the aristocrats. But on his death some of the glamour and glitter had gone from the city.

However, Sheldon thought, everything was working out as he had anticipated, and as he was heartily sick of being shut up in his room he decided it would be foolish to refuse Lady Imogen's invitation.

The very comfortable carriage, which had been built for the Dowager Marchioness so that despite her arthritic legs, which left her almost crippled, she could travel from London in comfort, was really unnecessary.

Dr. Price had been delighted to see how quickly Sheldon's wound was healing.

After all, he had only received a glancing blow from the bullet, which he learnt from Chapman had finally embedded itself in the cushioning at the back of the Chaise.

Not only was Bobo a skilful valet, having at times looked after the *Duc*, but Chapman was exceptionally proficient in giving a boot the iridescent polish which fashion decreed was essential.

With the help of Francine, who washed and ironed his shirts and handkerchiefs, Sheldon enjoyed a degree of comfort that he had not experienced since he had last been in England.

'Then' he thought, 'when I lived at home . . .'

He checked himself abruptly.

What was the point of thinking back into the past? The less of the past both he and those in Bath remembered, the better!

Despite the fact that his arm was in a sling and he had to wear his coat hanging from one shoulder, he looked exceedingly elegant and outstandingly handsome as he walked down the stairs of the Hotel with Cerissa at his side.

Dressed in black velvet trimmed with white ermine and carrying an ermine muff, she looked so lovely that even the flunkeys on duty stared at her with undisguised admiration.

It had not escaped the notice of the Receptionist that the Dowager Marchioness's carriage was waiting outside, and Sheldon and Cerissa were bowed into it with a deferential politeness that was almost reverent.

"Francine says they are extremely proud to have you in the Hotel now that you are such a hero," Cerissa said as the carriage started off.

"I am not interested in laurel leaves," Sheldon replied. "At the same time, I must congratulate you, Cerissa, in having manoeuvred your way extremely skilfully into an advantageous position."

He did not sound very congratulatory and Cerissa moved a little closer and slipped her hand into his.

"I am so excited at going out with you," she said, "and that we are going to a party together."

"Sir Ralph will be waiting for you."

Sheldon's voice was cold, but almost automatically his fingers had tightened over Cerissa's.

"It is exciting! Say it is exciting!" she pleaded.

"The charade?" Sheldon questioned.

"We are deceiving everyone and being very clever about it!" she said. "But if you do not enjoy the pretence, then everything will be spoilt!"

Sheldon laughed as if he could not help himself.

"You are making it into a nursery game but it is more serious than that."

"I know, I know!" Cerissa answered. "But I love you when you laugh, and when your eyes twinkle! When you look severe and lecture me, it is like being covered by a black cloud."

Sheldon laughed again.

"I will try not to be gloomy," he promised.

"And say that it is fun, *très amusant,* that we are deceiving these stupid people, who have no idea that we are not who we are pretending to be."

"Do not boast! We must never underestimate the enemy."

"That is just what they are!" Cerissa said excitedly. "The enemy! And we shall defeat them all and be rich . . . *très riches* . . . both of us."

Sheldon did not answer, but he did not take his hand from hers until they reached Queen's Square.

It was only when he met Lady Imogen's eyes that he realised all too clearly that there was trouble ahead.

The luncheon was delicious and Sir Ralph was obviously anxious to ingratiate himself with Cerissa's Guardian.

It was in a mood of mellow good humour, to which the excellent wines had contributed, that they left the Dining-Room for the white-and-gold Salon.

"Come and sit by the fire," Lady Imogen said to Sheldon. "You must rest comfortably, otherwise I shall feel that Dr. Price will rebuke me for letting his patient do too much too soon."

Sheldon did as he was requested and Lady Imogen seated herself near him so that if they kept their voices low he knew their conversation would not be overheard by Cerissa and Sir Ralph.

He was showing her a folder which contained pictures of old Bath and drawings of Prior Park—a magnificent private house on the outskirts of the city, which had been built by John Wood, who was responsible for so many other fine buildings.

Their voices only reached Sheldon in a murmur, and Lady Imogen, as if to draw attention to herself, said softly:

"I have been looking forward to meeting you ever since I saw you being carried upstairs looking like a Roman Centurion."

Sheldon did not answer and after a moment she said:

"But now I think we have met before."

"You were very young," he answered, "and already London was talking of little else but your beauty."

"You flatter me, but I hope I have improved with age."

"What can I reply to that? Except to say that a flower in full bloom is invariably at its best!"

Lady Imogen reached out her hand and laid it on his.

"Sheldon—as we are old friends I hope I may call you that—what have you been doing these past years?"

"I have been living in France."

She gave an affected little sound.

"Alas, there are so many beautiful women there that you must find it hard to exchange such exotic orchids for the English daisy."

"I would hardly describe you as a daisy!"

"And how would you describe me?" Lady Imogen asked softly.

"You must not try my flights of fancy too high," he answered. "Besides, from all I hear, you have a great number of admirers who have come from London with no other intention except to throw their hearts at your feet."

Lady Imogen made an impatient gesture.

"They bore me!" she said. "Everyone in London bores me, and I thought I was bored with Bath until now!"

Sheldon did not pretend to misunderstand her meaning.

"As you have already realised," he said, "my time is fully occupied in being a nursemaid."

He spoke as if he found it a hardship, and there was a little glint in Lady Imogen's eyes as she said softly:

"Your alluring Ward will have no difficulty in finding someone to squire her and leave you free for other things."

Sheldon did not speak and after a moment Lady Imogen said:

"It is a pity that Sir Ralph, who is obviously infatuated with her, is not eligible."

With the greatest difficulty Sheldon prevented himself from sounding too interested and asked casually:

"What do you mean—not eligible?"

He realised with a sense of annoyance that Cerissa and Sir Ralph had left the Salon.

"I have known Ralph for many years," Lady Imogen said. "He is extremely wealthy, his family is noble, and he has one of the most charming houses I have ever visited."

Sheldon waited, almost anticipating the blow that was to come.

"Ralph was married when he was quite a young man," Lady Imogen went on. "His wife is still alive, but she is incurably insane!"

Sheldon had far too firm a self-control of himself to show that Lady Imogen's words affected him in any way.

"Poor fellow!" he said lightly. "Now tell me about yourself."

"I am still trying to find a solution for your Ward," Lady Imogen answered, "and in fact I think I have one."

"Cerissa is very young," Sheldon replied. "I have no wish for her to be pushed into matrimony just because I find her something of an inconvenience. I believe that the *Duc* has invested quite a lot of money in London and she certainly has a fortune in France when things settle down again. She can afford to wait and take her choice."

"But in the meantime," Lady Imogen said, "you and I will have to wait with her, and that, Sheldon, is something I shall find extremely inconvenient."

"Patience is a virtue."

"Not to me!" Lady Imogen retorted. "Frankly, I have no patience! When I want something I want it at once! A fire that is not stoked will soon die away and become nothing but ashes!"

The note of passion in her voice was unmistakable.

"You have not changed!" Sheldon smiled. "I remember people talking about your impetuosity. You married Kenridge on an impulse and I wonder whether, had he lived, he would have regretted it."

"You knew him?" Lady Imogen enquired.

"We were at Oxford together and were rather good friends, as it happens. But I was abroad when you married, and when I returned, for some reason I cannot recall, we did not come into contact with each other."

"That is why we must now make up for lost time."

"Because of the promise I gave to the *Duc* de Valence before he was executed, I must devote myself to Cerissa's interests. After all, she knows no-one in England except for me."

"That is something that can easily be remedied," Lady Imogen replied. "I will give parties for her and entertain the whole of Bath while we are here. When we return to London, you will find my hospitality is unsurpassed as far as the *Beau Monde* is concerned."

"You have an answer for all my difficulties."

But he did not sound as if he was convinced.

Lady Imogen suddenly clapped her hands together.

"I have it! I have the perfect solution!" she cried. "How stupid of me not to think of it before!"

"Think of what?" Sheldon enquired.

"Mama told me this morning that Perequine is arriving tomorrow."

She saw that Sheldon looked puzzled and explained:

"Perequine is my brother and as usual he is in trouble with his Trustees."

"What sort of trouble?"

"Perequine imagines that he has fallen in love with a very pretty little Opera dancer at Drury Lane.

She is in fact quite fascinating, but nothing like as beautiful as your *Comtesse!*"

Sheldon waited, his eyes on Lady Imogen's face.

"My father left a very sensible will where Perequine is concerned," she continued. "If he marries before he is twenty-one, his Trustees will not release his fortune until he reaches the age of twenty-five."

"I can imagine that keeps him in check."

"Unfortunately, he will be twenty-one in May, when he swears that he will marry this creature, whatever her name is, and actually there is nothing we can do to prevent him."

Imogen made a little gesture with her hands.

"That is what I thought until now, but the solution is obvious."

"I am afraid I do not see one," Sheldon remarked.

"Your Ward—the *Comtesse!* She is a thousand times prettier, more alluring, and certainly more intelligent than any Opera dancer who ever pirouetted behind the footlights!"

"I am not certain . . ." Sheldon began.

"Oh, please," Lady Imogen interrupted. "Do not be prejudiced against Perequine just because of what I have told you. He is no more in love with this 'bit o' muslin' than he has been with a dozen others. The only way to stop him from sowing his wild oats is to get him settled down with someone charming and well-bred."

Again Lady Imogen laid her hand on Sheldon's.

"We must work together, you and I, to make these two young people happy."

She thought that he did not look convinced and she said:

"You know as well as I do that there is no more important family than the Wychwoods in the whole country, and Perequine, when he comes into his money, will be a very wealthy man. His properties are too many for me to enumerate and, although he is a little wild, underneath it all he is a very charming person."

"If he is like you he must be!"

"I knew you would see sense," Lady Imogen cried triumphantly.

"I have no wish to play the heavy Guardian," Sheldon said, "but after what you have told me about Sir Ralph I think we should find out what is keeping them so deeply engrossed elsewhere."

As if the words conjured them up, the door opened and they came back into the Salon together.

"We have been looking at your King Charles spaniels," Cerissa explained to Lady Imogen. "They are the sweetest dogs imaginable! Sir Ralph has said that he will give me one when I have somewhere to keep it."

She looked at Sheldon as she spoke.

"Sir Ralph obviously wishes to be generous," he said coolly, "but as you well know, we have not yet found a house where we shall live, and I have always thought that a dog is useless unless one looks after it one's self."

"I thought you would say that," Cerissa said a little sadly, "but perhaps later, when we leave Bath."

"When you do that, I am hoping you will both come and stay with me in Oxfordshire," Sir Ralph said quickly.

"I am sure we would love to do so," Cerissa replied impulsively.

"We are at present unable to make any future plans," Sheldon said coldly, "and now I think we should return to the Hotel."

"You are feeling tired?" Cerissa asked.

"A trifle."

"Then we will leave at once."

"You are coming again tomorrow," Lady Imogen interposed. "I am giving a special party tomorrow evening when my brother arrives in Bath. I will invite a lot of young people to meet him, but you, my dear *Comtesse*, will undoubtedly be the *Belle* of them all!"

Cerissa dropped her a polite curtsey.

"Thank you for a most enjoyable luncheon, My Lady. I shall look forward to tomorrow evening."

"And so, I hope, will your Guardian. His wound will be better by then, but you must make him rest so that he does not have to leave too soon after dinner."

"I will certainly try," Cerissa promised.

Sheldon raised Lady Imogen's hand to his lips.

"I see I have no say as to what we shall do and not do," he murmured in a low voice.

"None!" she replied. "And tomorrow morning I intend to collect the *Comtesse* and show her the Assembly Rooms."

"You are kindness itself!" Sheldon remarked.

"That is what I wish to be to you both," she answered, and there was a meaning in her words which he could not mistake.

Lady Imogen's carriage was waiting for them and as they drove away Sheldon realised that Sir Ralph was standing on the steps looking at Cerissa.

He had an expression in his eyes which revealed his feelings all too clearly.

Sheldon sat back in the carriage and said in a sharp tone:

"You have been wasting your time!"

"What do you mean?"

"Trevellyan is married!"

He felt Cerissa stiffen beside him. Then she said:

"It is impossible! How could he . . ."

She stopped.

"Now I understand some of the things he said. But where is his wife?"

"She is incurably insane!"

"*Non, non!* Poor Sir Ralph! I am so sorry for him!"

"And of course for yourself!"

"Not really. Just now I decided that although he was very kind I would not really wish to marry him."

"You are sure of that? Why this sudden *volte-face?*"

"I am not really sure," Cerissa said. "It is just that when we were looking at the puppies he touched my hand, and somehow, although I did not expect to, it made me shiver!"

"Nevertheless, if he had been free you would have married him?"

"I might. As his wife I would certainly be very respectable, *n'est-ce pas?*"

"You would. But a wedding-ring is something which he cannot offer you."

"I do not think he would dare to offer me . . . anything else . . . but still, some of the things he said . . ."

"What do you mean—things he said?" Sheldon interrupted abruptly.

"He told me that the moment he saw me he thought I was the most beautiful person he had ever seen; like a dream that had always been at the back of his mind, but which he never expected to materialise."

"How delightfully sentimental!" Sheldon sneered.

"He meant it. He was very serious, and yet now I understand why I knew he was suffering."

"He should have explained about his wife from the very moment he started dancing attendance on you."

"He has never mentioned her. Do you think he might have offered me . . . other than . . . marriage?"

"I doubt if he would dare to do so unless he had a shrewd idea of our real circumstances," Sheldon replied. "Of course there is always that possibility."

"You mean, if he guessed that we were penniless and that you had some . . . secret of which you will not speak?"

"Even then to suggest that he might become your protector would be an insult that would compel me to call him out."

"I thought duelling was forbidden in England."

"Officially it is, but no-one takes any notice of that law!"

"I would not wish you to . . . fight over me," Cerissa said. "You might be . . . hurt."

"I would be much more likely to hurt my opponent," Sheldon said dryly. "I may inform you that I have fenced with the best Masters in Paris and am considered a crack shot!"

"So there are two more accomplishments for which I must admire you," Cerissa said.

"It is not important what you feel about me," Sheldon retorted. "Do you know why Lady Imogen is giving a party tomorrow evening?"

"I imagine so that she can see you!"

Sheldon looked at Cerissa sharply. He had not expected her to be so perceptive.

"She is giving it so that you can meet her brother, the Marquess of Wychwood, who has been sent to Bath because he is making a fool of himself in London over an Opera dancer."

"And you are hoping that he will make a . . . fool of himself over me?"

"If you become the Marchioness of Wychwood," Sheldon said, "your position would, short of Royalty, be unequalled in English Society."

"I would like that."

"The Wychwoods have vast Estates, a country house in Hertfordshire, and a Mansion in London that is as magnificent as Carlton House."

"It sounds everything that I have ever wanted," Cerissa sighed.

"Then it should be easy, unless Wychwood is blind!"

"Perhaps he is so desperately in love with his Opera dancer that all other women pale into insignificance."

"What do you know about love?" Sheldon asked.

"I know that once one is really in love no-one else . . . exists in the whole . . . world."

"Who told you that nonsense?"

"It is not nonsense! It is what Papa felt for Mama

105

and she for him. It is what I know in my . . . heart I should feel if I ever fell . . . in love."

"Then for God's sake get married first!" Sheldon ejaculated.

"Perhaps I shall feel it for the man I marry."

"That sort of luck only exists in fairy-stories. Let me make it quite clear, Cerissa: you have chosen your path and you must not deviate from it. Marriage to a rich man—a ring on your finger—is your goal. It is no use expecting all that and Heaven too!"

"So you admit that being in love would be Heaven!" Cerissa asaid softly.

"I have not said so."

"But you know it is the truth. Could there be anything more wonderful than being close to someone you love . . . to touch them . . . to kiss them . . . to know that nothing else in the world was of any . . . importance?"

"Will you stop talking such moonshine?" Sheldon said angrily. "You have been reading some ridiculous novelettes which are blinding you to the harsh realities of life."

"I am not blind to what you call the harsh realities," Cerissa replied. "But neither they nor you can stop me from . . . dreaming or prevent me from knowing in my . . . heart what love is . . . like."

She spoke with a note in her voice which was like a throb and which told him that she was deeply moved.

Then before he had a chance to reply the carriage drew up outside the White Hart.

* * *

Sheldon lay down in the Sitting-Room and only when he was comfortable on a sofa in front of the fire and with a rug over his knees did Cerissa reveal that Sir Ralph had asked them to dine that evening.

"You will send a note to him refusing his invitation," Sheldon ordered.

He thought that Cerissa might argue with him,

and, because he was in fact feeling rather tired not only by the expedition to Lady Imogen's house but by the many problems which had arisen while he was there, he closed his eyes.

Cerissa stood looking at him uncertainly before she went to the writing-desk and wrote a note to Sir Ralph.

When she had finished, Bobo was told to deliver it, and when he had left the room Cerissa sat down on the floor beside the sofa on which Sheldon was resting.

Although he kept his eyes closed she was aware that he was not asleep.

After a moment she said in a low voice:

"Suppose we . . . change our plans? Suppose we could find enough . . . money to live on without my . . . having to get . . . married?"

"Are you really thinking of giving up your quest so quickly?" he asked. "We have not yet explored half the possibilities of Bath."

"Yesterday I thought that if he asked me I might marry Sir Ralph," Cerissa said in a low voice, "but today when he touched me I knew it would be impossible."

"I have already explained to you that you are asking too much," Sheldon said. "It is your own idea, Cerissa, that you must be respectable, that you must have a wedding-ring on your finger. What is making you hesitate on what might be the very brink of success?"

"I had wanted to have an . . . assured position . . . to be married and have everyone . . . respect me," Cerissa murmured in a low voice. "I had not . . . really thought what would happen when I was . . . alone with my . . . husband . . . like this."

"In your country, marriages are arranged," Sheldon said. "You are well aware that if your father had been able to acknowledge you as his daughter you would have been married by now to some young aristocrat and would have had little or no say in the choice."

"Yes, I know that," Cerissa agreed, "and perhaps, like poor Papa, I would have been married to someone dull and complaining, whom in time I would actively dislike."

"That is the luck of the draw," Sheldon said in a hard voice.

Cerissa did not speak and after a moment he went on:

"You, on the other hand, can pick and choose your husband, as long as our money lasts."

He gave a sigh.

"Instead of lying here I should be at the gambling-tables."

He threw the rug off his knees and sat up.

"No, no!" Cerissa cried. "You are tired. Wait until tomorrow."

"When it comes to making money, there is no time like the present!"

He got to his feet and walked across the room.

"Let me come with you?" Cerissa begged.

She ran after him and as he reached the door of the Sitting-Room she caught hold of his arm.

"Please . . . let me come with you?"

"No!" he answered. "Stay here and remember that the more money I make the longer you will have to pick yourself a suitable husband."

He went from the room and very slowly Cerissa returned to the fire.

Automatically she picked up the rug which Sheldon had thrown onto the floor, then cradled it in her arms.

"Mon Dieu!" she whispered beneath her breath. "Why am I so . . . foolish?"

*   *   *

The Chaise drove up to the Library and Sheldon stepped out.

There were quite a number of gentlemen seated

on the comfortable chairs in the centre of the room.

Sheldon picked up the *Times* and the *Morning Post* and, finding an empty chair, opened them with a little difficulty.

Although he managed with Chapman's and Bobo's help to wear a coat over his injured arm, he still carried it in a sling and found that it hurt him if he moved it quickly.

However, he intended to read the news.

He had finished with the *Times* and thrown it down on the floor before he picked up the *Morning Post,* when an elderly gentleman in the next chair spoke to him.

"I believe, Sir," he said, "you are that splendid fellow who disposed of the highwaymen three days ago."

"That is true," Sheldon answered.

"I would like to thank you," the gentleman said. "They robbed me last year of fifty guineas in gold and all the jewelry I was wearing."

"That was regrettable!" Sheldon remarked.

"It was indeed. My name is Walburton. I was giving a dinner-party on the night you arrived."

"I heard about it later, My Lord, but I was not in a position to take much notice at the time."

"So I learnt," Lord Walburton said. "It was a very courageous action on your part and one which, I assure you, is much appreciated amongst those of us who suffered at those criminals' hands."

"I should have thought something could have been done about it before now," Sheldon remarked.

"All the City Council is interested in is building," Lord Walburton remarked, "and raking in the money which is spent at the Baths."

"I suppose that is understandable," Sheldon said with a smile.

"It is no thanks to the modern planners if the water is hot," Lord Walburton retorted. "I have said over and over again—"

He stopped suddenly.

Barbara Cartland

"We must talk about it some other time, for I see now that you wish to read the newspapers."

"I was wondering," Sheldon said, "how it is possible to get the London papers here so quickly."

"That is entirely due to Palmer's mail-coaches," Lord Walburton replied. "They make the journey between here and the Capital every day."

"Is that possible?" Sheldon asked. "I thought perhaps they went once or twice a week."

"No, every day," Lord Walburton confirmed.

"Then I suppose," Sheldon said tentatively, "that some of the items of news from Bath now reach the London newspapers."

"You are quite right," Lord Walburton told him. "In the old days when I first came to Bath it was like going to a foreign country. One was cut off from everything except local gossip, and when I returned to London no-one had the slightest idea of what was going on here. But now things have changed."

"It was rather what I anticipated," Sheldon said almost as if he spoke to himself.

He rose to his feet and laid the *Morning Post*, which he had not opened, down on a chair.

"You are a hero in Bath, Mr. Harcourt," Lord Walburton said, "and I do not mind betting that they will have heard of your exploits in London when you get back there."

Sheldon did not reply. He merely bowed to His Lordship, but as he left the Library there was a deep scowl on his forehead.

* * *

The party given by Lady Imogen the night before had been an unqualified success. In fact the whole day had been successful.

Having won a few pounds the previous evening at the gaming-tables and returned to Cerissa in quite a good mood, Sheldon had, in his own words, "made a killing" the following afternoon.

He had sent Cerissa, despite her protestations,

110

The Heart Triumphant

for a drive with Francine, refusing to entertain several ardent suggestions from Sir Ralph.

He also insisted that there was no reason for her to appear in the Assembly Rooms, and she should keep quiet until the evening.

He had come back to change at the White Hart in such high spirits that Cerissa's eyes were shining and she was chattering excitedly long before they reached Queen's Square.

Lady Imogen had kept her word and the guests at dinner were young and attractive. There was a collection of girls to amuse her brother.

But, as she had anticipated, the Marquess took one look at Cerissa and was bowled over by her appearance.

It was not surprising, for Sheldon had chosen her gown with care.

Instead of black, which she had worn ever since she arrived in Bath, she was in a gown of dead white, which made her look very young. At the same time, it had a sophisticated elegance which only Paris could impart.

Her mother's diamond brooch glittered in her dark hair and she carried in her mittened hands an exquisitely painted fan.

She looked so beautiful that Sheldon was aware that there was a speculative look in Lady Imogen's blue eyes, and with an awareness that it could possibly spell danger he set himself out to disperse it.

He was successful over dinner, and when a four-piece orchestra started to play in the Salon so that the young people could dance, Lady Imogen drew him into her private Sitting-Room.

The scene had already been set, Sheldon realised, with softly shaded lights, a warm fire glowing in the hearth, and a sofa arranged with satin cushions directly in front of it.

As he closed the door behind them Lady Imogen melted into his arms and he kissed her as he was

111

expected to do, with a demanding insistence that was for the moment more a calculated precaution than a physical urge.

"I have been waiting for this," Lady Imogen murmured.

Words seemed unnecessary and Sheldon kissed her again.

He realised that she was extremely passionate.

Women with fair hair and blue eyes were generally supposed to have a cold temperament, but he had found they could also be consumed by raging fires of passion.

Lady Imogen gave a little sigh and drew him towards the sofa.

"Everything is going perfectly. Just as I planned it. Already Perequine has been captivated by Cerissa's beauty."

"They are both very young," Sheldon said, feeling that some answer was expected.

"While you and I are older and need waste no time in questioning what the fates have sent us."

She drew his head down to hers again and the exotic scent she used and the movements of her body against his were all too familiar.

However, she was unpleasantly surprised when Sheldon disentangled himself from her white arms and rose to his feet.

"We are going back to the Salon," he said in an uncompromising voice.

"Why, Sheldon? Why?"

"I would not wish Cerissa to think me anything but conformable," he answered.

Then as he saw a spark of anger in Lady Imogen's eyes, he said with that mocking note in his voice that she was beginning to mistrust:

"I have also an inescapable predilection for doing my own hunting."

For a moment he thought she would rage at him. Then she laughed.

"Always the unexpected!" she exclaimed. "I might

have guessed that you would be different from any man I have ever known."

"Let us keep it that way, so that you will not be bored too soon."

He straightened his cravat in the mirror over the mantelpiece.

"I am not bored with you," Lady Imogen said behind him. "When shall I see you again?"

"I will let you know."

"Tomorrow?"

"I am not yet certain of our plans."

"You mean it depends on your Ward. I will arrange for Perequine to take her driving."

"That may be possible, but she will not go unchaperoned."

Lady Imogen laughed as if she could not help it.

"I learnt that her maid came with her when Ralph brought her here the first evening."

"Cerissa is French," Sheldon said, "and French *jeunes filles*, as you well know, are brought up extremely strictly. There is no possible chance of my allowing Cerissa to be alone with a man until she is married."

"Set a thief to catch a thief," Lady Imogen murmured.

"We will go back to the Salon."

"What you are saying to me," she said as he began to move towards the door, "is that only when the *Comtesse* is married, or perhaps engaged, will you be free to do as I wish."

"You are putting words into my mouth," Sheldon protested. "What I really said is that it is hard to make plans when one has a very young and innocent girl to consider."

"The sooner she ceases to be both, the better!" Lady Imogen answered sharply.

"I do not intend to force Cerissa up the aisle."

He touched the handle of the door as Lady Imogen pulled him round to face her and once again her arms were round his neck.

"I will help you. I will help you, Sheldon, but do not make me wait too long."

Her lips were on his.

Then when she believed it would be impossible for any man to resist her, he firmly set himself free and they were walking back along the passage towards the Salon.

* * *

Sheldon drove from the Library to the Assembly Rooms, where he had arranged to meet Cerissa.

If she was happily occupied, he would go to the Card-Room; if not, he would escort her back to the Hotel. He told Chapman to wait.

Sheldon found Cerissa with several ladies whom she had met at Lady Imogen's party having tea with their daughters.

They had, however, been joined a few minutes before by the Marquess of Wychwood.

Sheldon had thought last night that the young Marquess looked exactly as he had expected.

He had fair hair and blue eyes, like his sister, but without her good looks, his countenance somewhat spoilt by a receding chin.

He was however dressed as befitted a "Tulip of Fashion" and had a natural gaiety that was undoubtedly attractive to women.

Sheldon was quite certain that he would find Bath exceedingly dull, and if she was to prevent him from returning to the allurements of the Opera dancer, Cerissa would have to act quickly.

There was no doubt that for the moment the Marquess was finding her as captivating as any "bit o' muslin."

He had eyes for no-one else in the party and appeared not to hear any remarks that were made to him by the other girls or even by their mothers.

As Sheldon approached them the Marquess turned round in his chair to look at Cerissa, making it very obvious that she was the only person in whom he was interested, and as far as he was concerned, no-one else existed.

Sheldon walked up to Cerissa and touched her shoulder.

There was a smile on her lips and her eyes lit up at the sight of him.

She jumped to her feet.

"You have been quicker than I expected, *Monseigneur!*"

"I feel quite confident that you have not missed me."

Sheldon bowed to the ladies with a grace which they found most attractive, then said to Cerissa:

"I think I must drive you to the Hotel. I have an urgent appointment in the Card-Room."

One of the ladies who overheard what he said gave a little cry.:

"Oh, please keep away, Mr. Harcourt," she begged. "You will bankrupt our poor husbands. I declare since you arrived in Bath their pockets are to let!"

"I assure you that compared with London, we do not gamble high," Sheldon said soothingly. "In fact the stakes are exceptionally low."

"It is low only for the winners," the lady replied. "It is the losers who complain."

"That is indubitably true," Sheldon answered. "Nevertheless, I find the cards irresistible, and so I must take my Ward home."

"May I accompany you, Sir?" the Marquess asked.

Sheldon raised his eye-brows as if he found the suggestion somewhat strange.

After he and Cerissa had said good-bye to the assembled company they walked through the magnificent rooms with their high ceilings and enormous crystal chandeliers towards the main entrance.

The Chaise was waiting in the forecourt.

"Do you intend to drive with us, My Lord?" Sheldon asked the Marquess.

"If you will allow me," the Marquess said eagerly. "The *Comtesse* has promised to show me some snuff-boxes which she brought from France. As I expect you know, Sir, my father's collection is world-famous."

"I have heard of it," Sheldon said cautiously.

"I have started a collection of my own."

As he spoke the Marquess drew from his pocket an exquisite snuff-box of gold embellished with enamelling and small diamonds.

"Oh, how pretty!" Cerissa exclaimed. "I have never seen anything so exquisite!"

"It is yours!" the Marquess said.

Sheldon took the box from Cerissa's fingers and handed it back to the Marquess.

"It is a pretty trinket," he said, "but my Ward is not allowed to accept presents of such value, as I am sure you are well aware."

There was a rebuke in his voice which made the Marquess look somewhat uncomfortable.

"I apologise," he said. "I spoke without thinking."

"It is understandable," Sheldon remarked good-humouredly. "And now tell me, what are your plans? How long do you intend to remain in Bath?"

"I meant to stay only a day or so," the Marquess answered, "but now I am in no hurry to leave!"

His eyes were on Cerissa's as he spoke, but she was looking out the window and seemed to have missed the implication behind his words.

It was only a short distance to the White Hart, and the Marquess followed them up the staircase to their private Sitting-Room.

"Wait here," Cerissa said. "I will fetch the snuff-boxes to show you."

She went into the bed-room, leaving Sheldon and the Marquess alone.

He looked at the young man before he said:

"My Ward is very young and has been very strictly brought up. She has never before met anyone like Your Lordship in the whole of her sheltered life."

The Marquess was listening but he looked puzzled.

"As one man of the world to another," Sheldon continued with a little twist of his lips, "I am asking you not to break her heart."

There was no mistaking the look of excitement in the Marquess's face.

"Do you think I am capable of doing that?"

"Only Cerissa can answer that question," Sheldon replied, "but I would not wish her to be unhappy."

"Nor would I, Sir! That I promise you!"

The note of sincerity in the Marquess's voice was unmistakable.

Sheldon put his hand on the young man's shoulder.

"Thank you," he said. "I knew you would understand."

When Cerissa came back into the room, Francine followed her, carrying some of the snuff-boxes.

She set them down on the table, then respectfully withdrew to a hard chair in the far corner of the Sitting-Room.

There she took up her sewing while the Marquess and Cerissa examined the snuff-boxes in front of the fire.

Sheldon looked at the homely scene. Then as the cynical lines from his nose to the corners of his mouth seemed to deepen, he left for the card-tables.

Chapter Six

"I must see you alone!"

"My Guardian will not allow it."

Cerissa moved gracefully through the more complicated steps of the minuet.

"We must contrive it somehow. You are driving me completely crazy!"

"Why should I be doing . . . that?"

The question sounded very young and artless.

"That is what I want to tell you," the Marquess said through gritted teeth.

Cerissa gave him a little glance from under her eye-lashes and realised that he was indeed frustrated.

It was not only on Sheldon's instructions that she had arranged that she should never be alone with him; it was also because she herself had no desire to hear the protestations of affection which she was well aware trembled on the Marquess's lips.

'There is no hurry,' she thought.

But the Marquess was becoming more and more importunate and she wondered if she could hold him at bay much longer.

As they danced sedately under the chandeliers in the Assembly Rooms, she knew that the Dowagers sitting round the walls were well aware of the Marquess's infatuation and had noticed that he never left her side.

It was really only a question of opportunity before his ardour was translated into words.

Cerissa was also almost certain that he would propose marriage.

Sheldon had not exaggerated when he told her of the Marquess's importance and that in becoming his wife she would achieve a position that any girl, especially one in her circumstances, would envy.

"There is plenty of time," she told herself.

She knew, however, that Sheldon was hurrying matters in every possible way. In fact, she felt she was being dragged willy-nilly to the altar.

She looked for Sheldon now across the crowded Ball-Room and saw him seated at the far end on a sofa beside Lady Imogen.

Their heads were close together and it was quite obvious that they were talking intimately.

The Marquess noticed the direction of her glance and said insistently:

"They are not troubling themselves about us. Let us slip away somewhere where I can have you to myself."

There was an eagerness in his voice and an expression in his eyes which made Cerissa feel uncomfortable.

She did not answer and after a moment the Marquess remarked almost peevishly:

"My sister is certainly more proficient at getting her man than I am at getting you!"

"What do you mean?" Cerissa asked.

"I would not be surprised if you woke up one morning to find that Imogen was your Guardian-in-law, or whatever the expression may be."

Cerissa stumbled over the next step of the minuet.

"Do . . . think . . . can you mean . . . ?" she stammered.

"I have never seen Imogen so ardent over any other man," the Marquess answered with a chuckle. "They usually chase after her, but where Mr. Harcourt is concerned it is a different story!"

Cerissa felt as if an icy hand clutched at her heart.

'So that is what Sheldon is contemplating!' she thought. 'Marriage to a rich woman . . . a woman who will be able to give him everything he wishes for in life.'

It seemed as if the Ball-Room swung round her dizzily and once again she stumbled.

The Marquess's hand tightened on hers.

"Are you all right?"

"I feel a little faint," Cerissa replied weakly.

They went to the side of the room, then through an arch-way into an Ante-Room where refreshments were being served.

The Marquess set Cerissa down on a comfortable chair and hurried to the buffet to bring her back a glass of lemonade.

She took it from him gratefully, feeling that her lips were dry and that despite the heat of the room she was suddenly very cold.

The Marquess seated himself beside her.

There were few people in the Refreshment-Room because everyone was dancing.

"Do you feel better now?" he asked.

"Much . . . better, thank you," Cerissa managed to say hesitatingly. "I . . . think we should . . . join your sister."

"There is no hurry," the Marquess said. "I want to tell you, Cerissa, what I feel. . . ."

"Not now . . . not here," Cerissa interrupted.

"Why not?" he asked. "I never get a chance at any other time, and I cannot sleep for thinking about you."

There was a note of passion in his voice which made Cerissa rise quickly to her feet.

"*Monseigneur* would be angry if I stayed here . . . alone with you."

"Damnit, he is not troubling his head about you at the moment!" the Marquess ejaculated.

But already Cerissa was moving towards the Ball-Room and he was forced to follow her.

Lady Imogen looked up when Cerissa and the Marquess came to her side. There was an expression in her eyes which it was impossible to misunderstand.

"Surely you two have not finished dancing already?" she asked crossly.

"Cerissa felt faint," the Marquess explained. "I do not blame her, the rooms are always too hot and too airless."

Sheldon looked at Cerissa before he asked:

"You are unwell?"

"I am all right . . . now," Cerissa answered.

She wondered frantically if he was as irritated as Lady Imogen was that their *tête-à-tête* had been interrupted.

She wondered what they had been saying to each other and whether, as the Marquess had suggested, they were in fact planning to be married.

Then before Sheldon could speak again Lord Walburton joined them.

"Good-evening, My Lady. Good-evening, Harcourt."

He nodded to the Marquess.

"I have a special bit of gossip for you, Lady Imogen," Lord Walburton said gleefully.

"What is it?" she smiled.

Lord Walburton was noted as being the most inveterate gossip in Bath.

"You remember D'Arcy Arbuthnot?"

"Yes, of course," Lady Imogen answered. "He was dining with me the other night."

"Well, at last he has caught his heiress!"

"He has?" Lady Imogen exclaimed.

"She is plain, thirty-five if she is a day, and as rich as Croesus!"

"He deserves his good luck. He has certainly been persistent!" Lady Imogen laughed.

"What is more, he is taking no chances," Lord

Walburton went on. "He was married this afternoon at the Octagon."

"Where is that?" Sheldon asked.

"It is the most famous of our proprietary Chapels," Lord Walburton explained. "There are six in all, built by private speculators more as a means of profit than of spiritual welfare."

"They are not consecrated but are entitled to perform 'Fleet marriages,'" Lady Imogen interposed, "which means that no licence, banns, or parental consent are required."

"I had no idea that such places existed in Bath!" Sheldon exclaimed.

"The marriages are perfectly legal," Lord Walburton replied, "but are expensive, and the Chapels attract large congregations by offering exciting preachers and good music."

"They are exactly like the Mayfair Chapel in London," Lady Imogen went on, "where the Duchess of Hamilton was married. I am glad for D'Arcy's sake that he can now relax and enjoy the luxury of a rich wife."

"He may have to shut his eyes," Lord Walburton smiled, "or else she can provide him with solid-gold-rimmed spectacles!"

There was a little unkind laughter at this. Then Lord Walburton said to Sheldon:

"By the way, Harcourt, I have some news for you too."

Sheldon raised his eye-brows.

"There was a half column about you in the *Times* of yesterday. I meant to tell you about it, but you will be able to read it in the Library."

"About his success in shooting the highwaymen?" Lady Imogen asked.

"His courage is much commended, and in an editorial the *Times* suggests that if all travellers were so enterprising we should soon rid the countryside of these pests."

"You see, Sheldon, you are famous!" Lady Imogen said, and there was a caressing note in her voice.

"I would like to go . . . back to the . . . Hotel," Cerissa announced suddenly.

Sheldon rose to his feet.

"I will take you."

"I told you these rooms are too hot," the Marquess said fretfully. "One might just as well be sitting in the hot baths!"

He put his hand under Cerissa's elbow to assist her across the room.

As she moved away she heard Lady Imogen say to Sheldon:

"Come back as soon as you have taken her to bed. I will be waiting."

He did not reply and walked on the other side of Cerissa.

Their Chaise was waiting in the forecourt and without asking permission the Marquess followed Cerissa into it and sat down on the small seat.

"You must rest," he said, "and tomorrow morning I will call to see if you would like to go driving."

"Thank you," Cerissa murmured.

When they stepped out after the short drive to the White Hart, Sheldon said to Chapman:

"I shall not require you any more this evening."

"Thank you. Good-night, Sir."

"Good-night, Chapman."

Cerissa felt her heart lift and the constriction in her breast was not as heavy as it had been in the Assembly Rooms.

They reached the Hall and she held out her hand to the Marquess.

"Good-night, My Lord."

"You will come out with me tomorrow? I must see you."

"It will be delightful . . . if I feel well . . . enough."

He held her hand very tightly in his. Then as if he could not help himself he raised her fingers to his lips.

"Remember that I must see you alone," he said in a low voice which only she could hear.

She took her hand from his and moved towards the stairs.

As she did so, Sheldon said to the Marquess:

"I want to talk to you. Will you wait here until I have seen my Ward to her room?"

"Of course."

Sheldon followed Cerissa up the stairs.

When they were out of ear-shot she asked:

"What have you to say to the Marquess?"

"I will tell you later."

She did not understand the expression in his eyes. Instinctively she was aware that something had happened; something which she felt without any clear reason was momentous.

They reached the door of her bed-room.

"What is worrying you?" she asked. "I must know. I cannot bear to be kept in ignorance."

"I have said that I will tell you later. Go to bed now!"

"You will come to me? You promise?"

"I will keep my word," he answered, and turned towards the stairs.

Cerissa stared after him with troubled eyes. Then, feeling apprehensive and worried, she went into her bed-room, where Francine was waiting for her.

The Marquess was standing in front of the big fire in the open Hall.

"Let us go into the Writing-Room," Sheldon suggested. "There is rarely anyone in there at this time of the night."

He did not wait for the Marquess to answer, but went into the small, rather sparsely furnished Writing-Room containing four desks and there were two arm-chairs in front of a dying fire.

Sheldon shut the door and walking to the hearth said:

"I thought it only fair to tell you that tomorrow Cerissa and I will be leaving for Scotland."

The Heart Triumphant

"For Scotland?" the Marquess ejaculated.

"I did not wish to distress Cerissa by telling her about it until after she had enjoyed this evening's entertainment, but is imperative that we should leave as early as possible."

"But Scotland! Why must you go there?"

"One of my relatives from whom I have considerable expectations is dangerously ill," Sheldon explained. "I can only hope that I may be in time."

"It is impossible!" The Marquess exclaimed. "I mean—must Cerissa go with you?"

Sheldon was still and there was silence until he asked slowly:

"Why exactly would you wish her to stay here?"

"I love her!" the Marquess replied. "I tried to tell her so tonight, but she would not listen to me."

There was a silence. Then Sheldon, again very slowly, said:

"You would think it very remiss of me if, as Cerissa's Guardian, I did not enquire what your intentions are."

There was practically no pause before the Marquess said quickly:

"I wish to marry her! There is of course no hurry, but I believe we will deal well together."

"I think so too," Sheldon agreed. "But where you are concerned there is in fact a great need for haste."

"Why should you say that?" the Marquess enquired curiously.

Sheldon smiled.

"Do you think I can take Cerissa practically the whole length and breadth of the country without at least a dozen men falling in love with her and asking her to be their wife?"

"I can understand that," the Marquess muttered. "She must be engaged to me before she leaves."

Sheldon shrugged his shoulders.

"Engagements are easily forgotten and—broken."

The Marquess's eyes were suddenly alert.

"What are you suggesting?"

125

"I am suggesting that if you love Cerissa, as I believe you do, you should marry her before she has a chance to find someone more to her liking."

"You mean—marry her before you leave for Scotland?"

"Why not?"

He saw the astonishment on the Marquess's rather stupid face and went on:

"I would not suggest this if I did not know that Cerissa's affections were deeply engaged; that is why I asked you to be careful not to break her heart. But now that I know you are serious in your pursuit of her, I see no reason why your marriage should be delayed."

"There are my Trustees . . ." the Marquess began.

"I understand from your sister that you are free of them in May, and anyway, is it likely that they would object to anyone as well-born as Cerissa?"

"No, of course not! Besides—" The Marquess gave a light laugh. "I think they would be very relieved that I was settling down, considering the trouble I have caused them this past year."

"I have no wish to press you," Sheldon said, "but even for a marriage as important as that of Cerissa, I cannot delay my departure from Bath tomorrow later than, shall we say, noon?"

"Then we must be married before you leave," the Marquess said as if the idea were entirely his own.

"I am sure you are wise to make that decision," Sheldon told him. "After all, it might be three or four months before you saw Cerissa again and we all know that 'out of sight means out of mind'!"

"We will be married!" the Marquess said firmly.

"If you are so determined," Sheldon said almost as if he himself were reluctant, "then I had best make the arrangements for you. I think it would be unwise for your mother or even your sister to know what is happening until Cerissa is legally your wife."

He paused before he added:

"And I know you will understand that I do not

wish to tell your sister of my departure. It will distress her and I cannot bear farewell scenes."

"I can understand that," the Marquess answered. "If you would be kind enough to make the arrangements, then all I need do tomorrow morning is to behave quite normally with my mother so that she will not be in the least suspicious."

"I will see the Parson at the Octagon, if that is the name of the Chapel, first thing in the morning," Sheldon said. "If he is not free to perform the ceremony, there are, as Lord Walburton said, a number of other Chapels."

He thought for a moment, then he added:

"Come to the Hotel at eleven A.M. Bring your own Phaeton, for I shall be leaving in my Chaise the instant the ceremony has been performed."

"I understand, and thank you," the Marquess said. "I am indeed very grateful!"

He held out his hand and Sheldon shook it.

"You will tell Cerissa what we have arranged?" he added. "I suppose it is too late for me to see her now."

"As she is a trifle indisposed," Sheldon answered, "owing as you so rightly said to the heat of the Ball-Room, I feel sure she will already be in bed. I will tell her first thing in the morning and I know how happy the news will make her. Apart from anything else, she is tired of travelling, poor child!"

"We will spend the first part of our honeymoon in Bath," the Marquess said, "then I will take her to London. She will certainly shine there! An Incomparable who will make all the others look like milkmaids!"

"You are quite right," Sheldon agreed. "Cerissa is an Incomparable amongst Incomparables, and you are a very lucky chap!"

"I am indeed!" the Marquess smiled. "And I am grateful now to my Trustees for not letting me marry that little Opera dancer. Nevertheless, she was an entrancing creature!"

"I am sure there are many attractive young women who will be heart-broken by your decision to enter into the bonds of holy matrimony," Sheldon said, and found it difficult to keep the mocking note from his voice.

The Marquess gave a light laugh.

"I am afraid there is quite a lot of truth in that!"

The two men left the Writing-Room together. In the Hall, the Marquess bade Sheldon good-night and walked towards the Hotel entrance.

"Not a word to your sister," Sheldon warned, "and will you convey to her my most abject apologies that I am unable to return to the Assembly Rooms to-night?"

"I will make your excuses," the Marquess said. "Imogen will not be pleased, but leave it to me."

He walked jauntily towards the front door while Sheldon turned towards the stairs.

"Conceited young pup!" he muttered to himself savagely.

He walked along the passage and knocked gently on the door of Cerissa's room.

"Come in!"

He entered to find that she was in bed.

The only light came from the fire and a candle burning by her bed-side.

She looked very lovely with her dark hair falling over her shoulders onto the white sheets, her eyes wide and apprehensive in her small heart-shaped face.

"What is it? What do you have to . . . tell me?" she asked as Sheldon stood looking at her.

He crossed the room to the fire to stand staring into the flames.

"You have pulled it off!" he said after a moment. "You are to marry the Marquess at noon tomorrow!"

"Marry . . . the Marquess? What . . . do you . . . mean? H-how . . . do you know?"

"Because I have arranged it. Walburton's tale of the proprietary Chapels was just what I wanted to hear."

"But there is no hurry. Why should I . . . do this?"

"Because I am leaving Bath immediately after your marriage."

"Why? Why? What has happened?"

"I am going to Ireland," Sheldon answered, "although incidentally I told your future husband that Scotland was my destination."

"I . . . I do not understand," Cerissa said in a frightened voice.

Sheldon did not answer her and she went on:

"I will not . . . marry anyone so quickly and in . . . such haste! It is . . . indecent!"

"It is something you have to do and you are extremely fortunate that I have been able to arrange it."

"Tell me why! You must . . . explain."

He seemed to hesitate and she cried frantically:

"I must know!"

"I will tell you."

He was still for a moment, as if choosing his words, before he said:

"The reason why I left England five years ago is that I killed a man!"

"I guessed it was something like that," Cerissa murmured. "Was it a duel?"

"It was a duel," Sheldon confirmed, "but unfortunately my opponent was my first cousin, the oldest son of my Uncle, the Earl of Donnington!"

"That is why Sir Ralph spoke of Donnington Park as being your family Mansion."

"It belonged to my grandfather and I was brought up there until I was fifteen. Then my Uncle inherited the title and my father and mother, who had lived with my grandfather when he was old and ill, had to find somewhere else."

"That was sad for you."

"My father disliked leaving, but there was nothing he could do. He was the second son and he had never got on with his older brother."

There was a pause before Cerissa prompted:

"Go on! Tell me what happened."

"My uncle had two sons, the oldest being Gervase, an exceptionally unpleasant child who did not improve with age. He always hated me, and I disliked him!"

Cerissa was listening intently, her fingers locked together, her eyes on Sheldon's face.

He did not look at her as he continued:

"Gervase took to drinking and in London he made a fool of himself in innumerable ways so that on many occasions I was ashamed to own him as a relative."

Sheldon drew a deep breath before he continued:

"One evening in White's he joined me at a table where I was gambling and proceeded to be offensive."

"What did he do?"

"He abused me, practically accused me of cheating, then repeated some slanderous and extremely insulting gossip about a lady in whom I was interested."

"You . . . loved her?"

"Shall I say that I was as enamoured as any young man might be of a beautiful woman who was older than himself."

"What . . . happened?"

"Gervase went too far and it was impossible for me in honour to do anything but challenge him."

"He . . . accepted your challenge?"

"We rose from the table to settle matters once and for all."

"*Hélas!* You decided to fight . . . there and then?"

"It was a moonlit night and we went into St. James's Park."

"Were you fighting with swords or pistols?"

"With pistols. Gervase had the choice of weapons and he considered himself to be a better shot than me."

Cerissa drew in her breath.

"What happened?"

"Gervase cheated," Sheldon answered, and his voice was hard.

"How . . . did he do . . . that?"

"He turned on the count of nine and fired while I still had my back to him."

Cerissa gave an audible gasp.

"Fortunately, he was too drunk for his aim to be accurate. It blew my hat from my head. I swung round and fired in return."

"And . . . killed him! But it was not your . . . fault!"

"That is what the Referee and all four seconds agreed, but my Uncle would not listen."

"You told him what had occurred?"

"I told him. I went to see him to express my sincere regret for what had happened, and I tried to explain that it was not my intention to do more than wing Gervase."

Sheldon straightened his shoulders as if he were on trial before he said:

"Had my cousin been standing as he should have been, the shot would have entered his arm and not his heart."

"Why would your Uncle not listen to the . . . truth?"

"He had always hated me and he told me that if I did not get out of England immediately he would inform the Magistrates that I had always intended to murder Gervase. He swore that he would give evidence to the effect that I had threatened his son's life on several occasions!"

"But that was a . . . lie!"

"Of course it was a lie!"

"But surely they would not have convicted you?"

"A trial at the Old Bailey would have caused a terrible scandal. It not only would have broken my mother's heart but would also have humiliated my father, who was very proud of the family reputation."

"It was cruel! Cruel of your Uncle to behave in such a fashion!"

"There was nothing I could do, except to leave

the country," Sheldon went on, "and he warned me that if I ever returned, a warrant would be issued for my arrest!"

"*C'est impossible* . . . unbelievable!"

"That is what my father said, but my Uncle meant every word of his threat."

"Is your father still alive?"

"No, he died two years ago."

There was silence, then Cerissa said in a very small voice:

"You . . . think that your Uncle . . . may have . . . you arrested now?"

"I am sure of it," Sheldon answered. "I thought coming to Bath that no-one in London would know that I had returned and that we could stay here in peace at any rate until you were married, but now . . ."

"You mean your Uncle will have . . . read about you in the . . . newspapers?"

"He will undoubtedly read the *Times*."

"But surely after all these years he will have . . . forgiven you?"

"He has never been known to forgive anyone."

"Then you must hide from him! You must save yourself!"

"That is what I intend to do," Sheldon replied, "by leaving for Ireland."

"You will be . . . safe there?"

"I imagine so, especially if you tell everyone that I have gone to Scotland. Perhaps later I shall go to America. I am told there are many opportunities in the New World."

"B-but . . . you cannot do that . . . you cannot . . . leave me!"

"You will be married! You will be the Marchioness of Wychwood. You will have everything in life you ever wanted: a wedding-ring, respectability, and a position of importance."

His lips twisted in the mocking smile she knew so well as he added:

"You will most certainly be inside the doors which matter and not outside them."

"But I . . . must see you . . . I cannot let you go like . . . this . . . I cannot live not knowing where you are and what is . . . happening to you."

"It is better this way," Sheldon said. "We met by chance, perhaps a lucky chance for us both. Certainly fortune is smiling on you."

"But I must . . . help you . . . I must . . . give you money. You cannot manage on the little you have."

"I have already doubled my fortune, such as it is, since I have been here," Sheldon answered. "Even after paying our Hotel bill I shall still have enough to enable me to sit down at the gaming-tables in Dublin without embarrassment."

Cerissa did not answer and he added:

"I will take Chapman with me for as long as I can afford him."

There was a finality about his words which made her cry out:

"But you cannot . . . go like this! You cannot . . . leave me tomorrow as if the time we have been together . . . meant nothing . . . as if it had not happened. . . ."

"We have achieved what we set out to do," Sheldon interrupted. "You will have a husband, albeit young and a little wild, but you are clever enough to manage him very competently."

"He is nothing but a tiresome, stupid boy!" Cerissa said petulantly. "I want a man who will look after me . . . a man to take care of me."

"The Marquess will be quite capable of doing that."

For almost the first time since he had been telling her his story, Sheldon looked at her, and there was a brutal note in his voice as he said:

"There is of course Sir Ralph, who would, I am sure, be willing to offer you his—protection."

Cerissa made a helpless gesture with her hands.

133

"For God's sake, be grateful!" Sheldon said sharply. "The Marquess is a better catch than I ever anticipated you might land, even with your looks!"

"I am . . . thinking about . . . you," Cerissa said in a low voice.

"Forget about me. I am able to take care of myself."

"What about . . . Lady Imogen?"

"What about her?"

"The Marquess thinks that she wishes to . . . marry you."

Sheldon laughed.

"I doubt it. Unlike you, her desires could never be requited by the placing of a ring on her finger."

"She . . . loves you!"

"You really believe that is—love?"

The cynicism in his words was all too clear.

"If you stayed here I could at least . . . see you. We would move in the same social circles."

"Do you really think that would be very satisfactory?" Sheldon asked ironically. "For my part, I would find it intolerable. No, Cerissa, your life in the future will be straight-forward, and I have no wish to complicate it."

"But you would not do that," Cerissa argued. "You would be there if I wanted you, and . . ."

"I have already said no!" Sheldon replied sharply. "Now I am going to bed. I must rise early to make arrangements for your wedding and make sure that all the wordly goods I possess are packed before the ceremony takes place."

He walked towards the door as he finished speaking.

"Sheldon! *Monseigneur!*" Cerissa cried. "*Ecoutez!* Listen to me! *Monseigneur* . . ."

But Sheldon did not look back.

He went from her bed-room and the door closed behind him.

"*Monseigneur!*"

Cerissa threw off the bed-clothes and made as if

to jump out of bed. Then suddenly she realised the hopelessness of trying to stop him.

She sat still where she was.

"I love him!" she told herself. "And after tomorrow I shall never see him again!"

She had known of her love for what now seemed to have been a long time, and yet she had forced herself not to acknowledge it, not to let her heart intrude upon the determination of her mind.

"I love him! I love him!"

Now the words seemed to beat against her as if someone else were saying them, repeating them over and over again until they drummed in her ears, growing louder and louder, until her whole body vibrated to the rhythm of it.

"I love him! *Je l'adore!*"

Though she had never told him, she thought he must have been aware that her heart turned over whenever he came near her, whenever their eyes met.

Perhaps that was why he had not looked at her while he was telling her the story of his exile and the danger he was now in.

He would have seen the love she felt for him shining in her face. Perhaps it might have made him hesitate before he decided to walk out of her life as unexpectedly as he had come into it.

Then she told herself that he did not care. He was not interested in her any more than he was really interested in Lady Imogen, who had so much to offer him.

She thought of Sheldon going to Ireland, disappearing over the sea to a country which she was never likely to visit and which she knew was very primitive.

"I shall never see him again," she whispered despairingly, and felt as if her whole future was dark, empty, and without hope.

"I loved him from the first moment I saw him!" she went on, and remembered how handsome he had appeared as he had risen from his seat in front of the open fire at the Hôtel d'Angleterre.

He had kissed her. At least she would have that to remember.

She admitted now that since then there had never been a night when she had not gone to sleep trying to recapture the feel of his lips on hers and the strength of his arms when he had held her against him.

That kiss had spoilt her, she thought wildly, because never again would it be possible for a man to touch her, even on the hand, without her feeling revolted by it, as she had been by Sir Ralph.

And tonight when the Marquess's mouth had touched her fingers, she had felt a cold shiver run through her veins almost as if his lips had been those of a reptile.

"He is only a stupid, brainless boy!" she told herself.

Then insidiously, frighteningly, the fact was borne in upon her that he was man enough to want more from her than a kiss!

There had been a look in his eyes as he had spoken to her in the Ball-Room which was impossible to misinterpret.

There had been the same vibrations emanating from Sir Ralph, and Cerissa was aware that she wanted desperately to keep the Marquess at arm's length.

If he approached her too closely she would want to run panic-stricken to safety!

And what did safety mean, ever since she had entered that private room in Calais, except Sheldon?

"I love him! I love him!"

Always she got back to the same drumming and throbbing within her heart, the same yearning which pervaded her whole body like an aching wound until she knew it was impossible to face life without him.

Once again Cerissa pushed aside the sheet and blankets and now she stepped out of bed.

Francine had left her négligée lying over a chair. Automatically she put it on and walked towards the door.

Even as she started to turn the handle she paused.

If she went to Sheldon, what could she say to him?

He did not want her; he could not afford to keep her; she knew that, as he had said to her once before, he would travel faster if he travelled alone.

"I should only be an encumbrance," she told herself.

Slowly she walked back to the fireplace.

Sheldon had arranged her life and she had little choice but to accept the Marquess and be thankful that he had so much to offer her.

It was the sort of marriage she had always prayed for, the respectability she had wanted, the wedding-ring on her finger which her mother had never possessed.

" 'The Marchioness of Wychwood!' " she thought.

"I will show those stuck-up aristocrats, who always looked down their noses at Mama and me, how little they matter!" Cerissa said triumphantly to herself.

Then she remembered that most of them were dead, their heads cut off by the slanting blade of the guillotine to fall into the blood-stained basket beneath it.

"Who am I impressing? Who cares what I do?" she asked aloud.

Her voice seemed to echo in the shadows of the room. Then she sank down onto the hearth-rug and began to cry.

Chapter Seven

Chapman drove the Chaise into the forecourt with a flourish and drew up outside the steps of the White Hart.

Sheldon jumped down before one of the servants could open the door.

He was late because he had been unable to persuade the Chaplain of the Octagon to cancel a previous engagement and had been forced to find another Chapel where Cerissa could be married.

He had finally located the Chaplain of St. Mary's, which was the oldest of the proprietary Chapels in Bath. Everything was now arranged, but it had taken him longer than he had expected.

As he ascended the steps he saw that Bobo was at the top of them beside his luggage. He would have passed with only a nod of his head had not Bobo moved quickly to prevent him.

"Get the luggage on the Chaise, Bobo," Sheldon ordered.

"Excuse me, *Monsieur*," Bobo replied in a low voice which could not be overheard by the other servants, "but there were two gentlemen enquiring for you a few minutes ago."

Sheldon was still.

"What did they look like?"

Bobo considered the question, his bright eyes on Sheldon's face.

"I think, *Monsieur*, they were Clerks of some

sort. One was elderly and one quite young. Well dressed, but *pas à la mode, vous comprenez?*"

"I understand exactly," Sheldon said in a hard voice. "Where are they?"

"As you were busy, *Monsieur*," Bobo replied, "I sent them away."

"Where to?"

"They asked me if *Monsieur* was staying here, and I told them that such a fashionable gentleman would be at the York House Hotel."

"That was clever of you, Bobo," Sheldon approved.

Then he hurried into the Hotel, thinking as he did so that Bobo doubtless knew as much about his affairs as he did himself!

It seemed incredible that the article in the *Times* should have produced such quick results, but he had no doubt in his own mind who the men enquiring for him were and who had sent them.

He had passed through the Hall and had reached the foot of the stairs when he saw the Marquess coming down them.

One look at the expression on his usually rather vacant face was enough to tell Sheldon there was something very amiss.

He waited until the Marquess reached him, then asked:

"What has happened? I regret being late, but I had difficulty in finding a Chaplain."

The Marquess's expression was one of despair mixed with incredulity as he replied:

"Cerissa has refused to marry me!"

"Refused?"

Sheldon's exclamation rang out like a pistol-shot.

"Yes, refused!" the Marquess repeated. "She says she does not love me."

Sheldon drew in his breath and with an effort forced a smile to his lips.

"And you believed her? My dear fellow, surely

139

you know that every woman on her wedding-day suffers from nerves and is frightened of taking the plunge into the sea of matrimony?"

"She was very positive," the Marquess said in a surly tone.

The two men had to draw to one side to allow one of the Hotel guests to pass them.

"We cannot talk here," Sheldon said. "Let us go into the Writing-Room."

They were fortunate to find the room empty and as Sheldon shut the door behind him he said:

"It is regrettable that I was not here when you called. But when I left this morning, Cerissa was exceedingly happy at the thought of marrying you."

"She is not happy about it now," the Marquess retorted.

"Of course not. Cerissa is very young," Sheldon replied, "and naturally this unseemly haste has proved disturbing. But she loves you, my dear man, and that is all that need concern you at the moment."

"Other women have always seemed very eager to become my wife," the Marquess said.

"Of course—you are a very presentable fellow and Cerissa finds you most attractive. But you must understand that it is always difficult for a *jeune fille* not to feel afraid of the man she is to marry just because he is—a man."

The Marquess preened himself a little.

"I realise that she is very inexperienced and innocent."

"That is why you have to be exceptionally gentle and understanding. Cerissa is not a 'bit o' muslin.' "

"You really think she will marry me?" the Marquess asked.

"I am sure of it!" Sheldon replied firmly. "I expect at this moment she is crying her eyes out because she thinks you have taken her seriously. Wait here while I talk to her."

"I would not wish to marry any girl who did not want me."

"Cerissa is not any girl," Sheldon corrected, "she is unique, a very beautiful and very sensitive young Frenchwoman, capable I am sure of deep emotions once she is awakened for the first time."

There was a smile on the Marquess's lips and a glint in his eye that had not been there before.

"Perhaps I was a little hasty in believing her when she told me she had changed her mind. But she sounded so positive!"

"You should have swept her into your arms," Sheldon declared. "Actions are always much more convincing than words!"

"You are right! Of course you are right!" the Marquess said in an excited tone.

Sheldon looked at the clock on the mantelpiece.

"The Chaplain is waiting for us," he said. "I will fetch Cerissa, and we must leave immediately."

His hand went out towards the bell-pull.

"Order yourself a bottle of champagne, my dear fellow. I think we could all do with a glass to fortify ourselves, and then there need be no more delays."

Sheldon did not wait to hear the Marquess's reply but left the room and went up the stairs two at a time.

He flung open the door of the Sitting-Room to find Cerissa standing at the far end of it, and he knew by the expression on her face that she had been waiting for him.

He slammed the door behind him.

"What the devil do you think you are doing?" he asked furiously.

"I . . . cannot . . . marry him!"

The words were hardly audible.

She wore an exquisite white gauze gown in which Sheldon, before he left the Hotel, had instructed Francine to dress her, but she had not put on the bonnet edged with lace or the velvet coat trimmed with fur.

The flames from the fire gleamed on her hair and seemed almost, despite herself, to lighten the sombre darkness of her eyes.

"You are marrying him and we are leaving at once for the Chapel!" Sheldon replied.

He glared at her across the room and there was a determination in his expression that was almost brutal.

"I . . . cannot and I . . . will . . . not marry the Marquess."

"Have you gone raving mad?" Sheldon demanded. "Can you not understand that this is an opportunity that may never come again? It is unlikely you will find anyone more important or more manageable than the Marquess."

He saw Cerissa's lips tighten as if obstinately, and he shouted furiously:

"Can you imagine that a man who was not a half-wit would marry a woman without knowing more about her than the Marquess knows about you?"

Cerissa did not answer and he went on:

"And supposing he makes enquiries? What do you think he will discover about an unknown French émigrée whom he is prepared to make his Marchioness?"

Cerissa turned her head away from him and Sheldon, now standing in front of her, ordered sharply:

"Look at me and listen!"

He waited and very slowly Cerissa raised her eyes to his.

"He would find," Sheldon went on furiously, "that the whole charade we have put on for his benefit was false and a lie!"

His tone was so violent that Cerissa made a little gesture with her hands as if in protest.

"You are not the *Comtesse* de Valence!" Sheldon said harshly. "Have you forgotten that you are in fact only the illegitimate daughter of the *Duc* who never married your mother?"

Cerissa gave a cry like that of an animal that has been hurt.

"Face facts, you little fool!" Sheldon went on.

"And thank the God above who has given you the opportunity of becoming respectable, of living the life you have always wanted!"

He paused as if for breath, and because his voice had echoed in its anger round the Sitting-Room, the silence, now that he was no longer speaking, seemed all the more poignant.

Cerissa's eyes were still on his.

She was very pale but she held herself proudly, and now slowly and distinctly so that he could hear every word she said:

"*Non!* I will not marry him . . . you cannot . . . make me!"

"Damnit!" Sheldon cried furiously, "you will marry him if I have to beat you unconscious and drag you to the altar."

He reached out his hands as he spoke and taking her by the shoulders shook her furiously. He asserted all his strength so that she was as helpless as a puppet in his hands.

As if his violence broke Cerissa's control, she cried:

"I love . . . you! . . . I . . . love . . . you! . . . How can I . . . marry another . . . man when I . . . love . . . you?"

The words came jerkily between her lips as Sheldon propelled her backwards and forwards.

Then as their implication struck him he stopped suddenly. His hands remained on Cerissa's shoulders but he was as still as if he had suddenly been turned to stone.

Her breath was coming in deep gasps and there were tears in her eyes, but she looked up pleadingly into Sheldon's face.

"I love . . . you. Let me . . . stay with . . . you. I will be . . . anything you . . . wish. Your . . . servant . . . your . . . mistress, but I . . . cannot leave . . . you."

She gave a sob that came from the very depth of her being as she whispered:

143

"I will ... work for ... you ... I will do ... anything ... you ask ... but I cannot ... let another ... man touch ... me."

The tears in her eyes overflowed and ran down her cheeks, but still her face, exquisitely lovely in its misery, was upturned to his.

Then, with an exclamation that was an agonised groan, Sheldon pulled her roughly into his arms and his mouth was on hers.

For a moment his kiss was so hard, fierce, and angry that the pain of it was almost unbearable.

Until as her lips were soft beneath his, as he felt her body move against him, his kiss became less violent but at the same time more demanding, more insistent.

It was as if they had both been starved of each other until now that the barriers between them were down they became indivisible.

Closer and closer Sheldon folded his arms round her until it was impossible for Cerissa to breathe, impossible to be aware of anything except that she was his and they were no longer two people but one.

She felt a rapture and a wonder streak through her which she knew was love. It was unlike anything she had known or even imagined.

The room round them, the world, and everything else ceased to exist and there was only Sheldon.

His lips drew her heart and soul from her breast and they were his and no longer belonged to her.

A flame rose in them both that seemed to leap higher and higher until it carried them into the burning heat of the sun itself.

Sheldon raised his head.

"Oh, my God," he cried. "How could you do this to me?"

"I love ... you ... *Je t'aime! J t'adore!*"

Cerissa was no longer pale: her cheeks were flushed and her eyes were radiant and shining as if every star in the sky was lost in their depths.

"My darling, my little love, my precious! I have tried to prevent this from happening, but you made it too difficult for me."

"I am . . . yours . . . I cannot . . . live without . . . you."

"You have to, my precious! Can you not understand, you have to!"

"Knowing that we . . . love each . . . other, how could I ever . . . think that . . . anything else mattered?"

She spoke with such a note of passion in her voice that Sheldon's arms tightened about her and instinctively his lips sought hers, only to check himself before his mouth took possession of hers.

"It is no use, my beautiful darling," he said. "They are looking for me. Bobo sent them away, but they will find me unless I leave Bath immediately."

"I am . . . coming with . . . you."

"I cannot allow you to do that. The Marquess is waiting for you downstairs."

"Do you really . . . believe that I could . . . marry him now?"

Her eyes were shining as she looked up at Sheldon and he felt as she had that they were encompassed by a splendid glory and everything else round them had disappeared.

"You will really come with me?" he asked hoarsely. "To exile, to poverty?"

He drew a deep breath before he said:

"If they catch me and I am convicted, I might be transported, or it would at least mean a long imprisonment."

"I will wait for you. I have waited all through . . . eternity to find you. Nothing . . . nobody can prevent me from loving you for the next . . . thousand years."

"My sweet, my darling! What can I say to you?"

"Tell me . . . what I want to . . . hear," Cerissa whispered.

"That I love you?" he asked. "You know that already. It has been an intolerable agony, a torture I cannot describe, to be with you and not to touch you and to give you away to another man."

"Which you have . . . failed to do."

"My sweet, are you sure? I could not bear you to regret making this sacrifice and later to reproach me."

"Do you think I would ever do that?"

He looked down at her face and thought he had never believed it was possible for a woman to look so happy, so shiningly, ecstatically radiant.

"You are right," he said quickly. "Nothing matters but our love and nothing else will ever matter."

His lips found hers, but as she vibrated against him and he felt a thrill run through her which made her whole body quiver, he took his arms from her.

"We must go," he said. "There is no time to be lost. Once we get away from Bath, we can make it difficult, if we are clever, for them to find me."

"Francine has already taken the luggage downstairs."

"You intended to come with me?"

"I meant to follow you . . . barefoot or on my . . . knees. Nothing you could have said or done would have . . . prevented me."

"My perfect darling," Sheldon said unsteadily.

Then as Cerissa reached towards her fur-lined cape which lay on a chair, there came a knock on the door.

Suddenly they were both rigid, their eyes seeking each other's.

The colour faded from Cerissa's cheeks and the lines on Sheldon's face seemed to deepen.

"Come in!"

He spoke even as Cerissa was wondering frantically whether they could escape by the bed-rooms.

One of the Hotel servants entered.

"Two gentlemen to see you, Sir," he announced.

Sheldon and Cerissa were facing the door. He felt a cold, trembling little hand slip into his and his fingers tightened on it.

Two men passed the servant and came into the room. The first, neatly and plainly dressed, was elderly with grey hair, followed by a younger man with pale eye-lashes which gave him the look of a ferret.

Both men advanced slowly until they reached Sheldon.

They bowed politely.

Sheldon did not speak and Cerissa felt her lips dry and her throat constricted.

"You are Mr. Sheldon Harcourt?" the elderly man enquired.

It was almost, Cerissa thought wildly, as if Sheldon were already in the witness box and the man facing him was the Prosecuting Counsel.

"I am."

"We understood you were abroad, Mr. Harcourt, and it was just by chance on opening the *Times* the day before yesterday that I read of your exploits in Bath."

Sheldon inclined his head.

If only he had allowed the highwaymen to rob them, he thought, the whole course of his life might have been altered.

"The article in the *Times* was very complimentary, Sir."

"So I believe," Sheldon remarked coldly. "I have not seen it."

"It was most fortunate, Sir, that I did so, since it enabled my Clerk and myself to avoid what might have been a very lengthy and difficult investigation considering we are at war with France."

"I can understand that."

"As it is, Sir, I am afraid you cannot be in time for the Funeral which takes place today, but you will undoubtedly wish to arrange a Memorial Service in a week or two."

"Funeral?" Sheldon asked. "Whose funeral?"

"Your Uncle, the Earl of Donnington, died of a heart-attack four days ago, and naturally we immediately tried to get in touch with you."

147

"Why?"

The elderly man looked surprised.

"You are, of course, your Uncle's heir. You are in fact, My Lord, the eighth Earl of Donnington."

For a moment it seemed as if Sheldon could not believe what he had heard. Then in a voice which sounded curiously unlike his own he asked:

"But my cousin, Richard—my Uncle's second son?"

"I am afraid that being abroad, My Lord, you have not been informed of your cousin's death over a year ago. A most regrettable accident."

"No, I did not hear of it."

Sheldon now had control of his voice.

"I can understand, My Lord, that this must all be a considerable shock, but you will appreciate it is important that you should attend to the many problems that have arisen from your Uncle's unexpected death."

The elderly man hesitated.

"I understood at the Reception-desk that Your Lordship was in fact leaving Bath today. May I ask that, if it is possible, you should repair to Donnington Park forthwith?"

"I am quite willing to agree to that."

The elderly man's face seemed to brighten.

"It will make things very much easier, My Lord, for all of us."

His eyes flickered for a moment towards Cerissa and then he said:

"Perhaps my Clerk and I should withdraw for a moment and give Your Lordship time to adjust your plans. We will wait downstairs until you send for us."

The two men bowed respectfully and went from the room. For a moment neither Sheldon nor Cerissa seemed capable of movement.

Then in a whisper he could hardly hear she said:

"Will . . . you still . . . want me?"

He turned and his arms went round her slowly

and gently, as if he realised already that there was no need for the frantic urgency with which he had held her before.

His lips were on her hair. Then he put his finger under her chin and turned her face up to his.

He saw by the fear in her eyes and by the trembling of her lips what she was thinking and he looked at her for a long moment before he said:

"You wanted to be respectable, my sweet."

"I shall ... understand if ... now you do not wish to ... marry an ... adventuress. All I ... ask is that I can ... stay with you ... that I can be ... near you."

Her voice broke on the words and she hid her face against his shoulder.

He held her against him before he said softly:

"I should be very lonely in Donnington Park without a wife to look after me."

He felt Cerissa draw in her breath and he added:

"Will you marry me, my adorable little adventuress? You may find it rather dull at times after all the excitements we have lived through! Respectability is dull, but perhaps we can endure it together!"

"Oh ... Sheldon!"

Cerissa was crying now and the tears were running down her face, but they were tears of happiness and glittered iridescently from the sunshine coming through the windows.

"I love ... you. I love ... y-you," she stammered. "Oh, *Monseigneur* ... I love you with .. all of me. *Mon chéri*, there is ... nothing else in the world but ... you."

His lips found hers and they clung together like two people who had escaped disaster and death by a hair's-breadth.

"You ... want me ... you really ... want me now that you have ... everything?" Cerissa whispered passionately against Sheldon's mouth.

"Do you think I want anything else?"

"It is true ... and we need no longer be ... afraid?"

Barbara Cartland

"You will be my wife, and I will guard and protect you until we die."

"That is . . . what I . . . longed for . . . the safety . . . I knew . . . only you . . . could give me . . . but you told me . . . I must . . . obey my mind . . . not my . . . heart."

"Yet you disobeyed me!"

"*Vous savez* . . . my mind was defeated . . . my heart triumphed!"

"In future you will obey me—and also behave with propriety!"

Cerissa looked at Sheldon from under her long eye-lashes, which were still wet, to see if he was serious.

"I must be . . . conformable . . . strait-laced, and . . . unemotional, like a real English . . . lady?"

"Like an English Countess—very correct!"

"*Hélas!* I think . . . I go back to France . . . it would be more amusing on the . . . guillotine!"

Sheldon laughed and pulled her against him.

"You cannot escape me, and if you try I really will beat you!"

"You are . . . *très impérieux!*"

The words were a caress more than an accusation.

"I am crazily in love and madly jealous!"

Cerissa drew in her breath.

"That is true . . . *vraiment?*"

She saw the answer in his eyes and murmured:

"I was so . . . jealous of Lady Imogen . . . *je déteste cette femme* . . . I wanted to strike her . . . to tear her eyes out!"

"Having seen you, how could I look at another woman?"

Sheldon's lips prevented Cerissa from replying. His kiss was fiercely, demandingly passionate and held her completely captive.

After a long time he raised his head.

"I want you! Oh, God, my little love, how much I want you!"

"And I . . . want you."

150

Again that provocative little glance.

"I am not English . . . but French . . . and *très passionnée!*"

With an effort Sheldon put Cerissa from him. Picking up her cape to place it round her shoulders, he handed her the bonnet which was lying beside it.

"Come," he said.

"We are going to London?"

"We are going to be married. The Chaplain is waiting, and as I have already paid the fee why should we waste it?"

Their eyes met and they began to laugh.

"Oh, *mon cher Monseigneur!* My wonderful . . . wonderful . . . Sheldon."

"My darling!"

Still laughing from sheer happiness, he put out his hand to take hers.

"After all, I am only an Earl," he said. "Are you quite certain you would not be wiser to accept the owner of a higher title who is waiting for you downstairs?"

"I am not interested in titles, or respectability, or even a . . . wedding-ring," Cerissa answered. "I know now there is only one . . . thing I want in . . . life."

"Which is?"

"*L'amour et toi,*" she replied. "Love and you. They are the same—*la même chose.*"

Their eyes met and for a moment all they could see was the flame of love leaping wildly and irresistibly.

Then masterfully Sheldon pulled Cerissa towards the door.

SPECIAL OFFER: If you enjoyed this book and would like to have our catalog of over 1,400 other Bantam titles, just send your name and address and 25¢ (to help defray postage and handling costs) to: Catalog Department, Bantam Books, Inc., 414 East Golf Rd., Des Plaines, Ill. 60016.

ABOUT THE AUTHOR

BARBARA CARTLAND, the celebrated romantic author, historian, playwright, lecturer, political speaker and television personality, has now written over 150 books. Miss Cartland has had a number of historical books published and several biographical ones, including that of her brother, Major Ronald Cartland, who was the first Member of Parliament to be killed in the War. This book had a Foreword by Sir Winston Churchill.

In private life, Barbara Cartland, who is a Dame of the Order of St. John of Jerusalem, has fought for better conditions and salaries for Midwives and nurses. As President of the Royal College of Midwives (Hertfordshire Branch), she has been invested with the first Badge of Office ever given in Great Britain, which was subscribed to by the Midwives themselves. She has also championed the cause for old people and founded the first Romany Gypsy Camp in the world.

Barbara Cartland is deeply interested in Vitamin Therapy and is President of the British National Association for Health.

Barbara Cartland

The world's bestselling author of romantic fiction. Her stories are always captivating tales of intrigue, adventure and love.

☐	THE TEARS OF LOVE	2148	$1.25
☐	THE DEVIL IN LOVE	2149	$1.25
☐	THE ELUSIVE EARL	2436	$1.25
☐	THE BORED BRIDEGROOM	6381	$1.25
☐	JOURNEY TO PARADISE	6383	$1.25
☐	THE PENNILESS PEER	6387	$1.25
☐	NO DARKNESS FOR LOVE	6427	$1.25
☐	THE LITTLE ADVENTURE	6428	$1.25
☐	LESSONS IN LOVE	6431	$1.25
☐	THE DARING DECEPTION	6435	$1.25
☐	CASTLE OF FEAR	8103	$1.25
☐	THE GLITTERING LIGHTS	8104	$1.25
☐	A SWORD TO THE HEART	8105	$1.25
☐	THE MAGNIFICENT MARRIAGE	8166	$1.25
☐	THE RUTHLESS RAKE	8240	$1.25
☐	THE DANGEROUS DANDY	8280	$1.25
☐	THE WICKED MARQUIS	8467	$1.25
☐	LOVE IS INNOCENT	8505	$1.25
☐	THE FRIGHTENED BRIDE	8780	$1.25
☐	THE FLAME IS LOVE	8887	$1.25

Buy them at your local bookseller or use this handy coupon:

Bantam Books, Inc., Dept. BC, 414 East Golf Road, Des Plaines, Ill. 60016

Please send me the books I have checked above. I am enclosing $_____ (please add 35¢ to cover postage and handling). Send check or money order —no cash or C.O.D.'s please.

Mr/Mrs/Miss_____

Address_____

City_____State/Zip_____

BC1—9/76

Please allow three weeks for delivery. This offer expires 9/77.

Barbara Cartland

The world's bestselling author of romantic fiction. Her stories are always captivating tales of intrigue, adventure and love.

☐	THE CRUEL COUNT	2128	$1.25
☐	CALL OF THE HEART	2140	$1.25
☐	AS EAGLES FLY	2147	$1.25
☐	THE MASK OF LOVE	2366	$1.25
☐	AN ARROW OF LOVE	2426	$1.25
☐	A GAMBLE WITH HEARTS	2430	$1.25
☐	A KISS FOR THE KING	2433	$1.25
☐	A FRAME OF DREAMS	2434	$1.25
☐	THE FRAGRANT FLOWER	2435	$1.25
☐	MOON OVER EDEN	2437	$1.25
☐	THE GOLDEN ILLUSION	2449	$1.25
☐	FIRE ON THE SNOW	2450	$1.25
☐	THE HUSBAND HUNTERS	2461	$1.25
☐	THE SHADOW OF SIN	6430	$1.25
☐	SAY YES, SAMANTHA	7834	$1.25
☐	THE KARMA OF LOVE	8106	$1.25
☐	BEWITCHED	8630	$1.25
☐	THE IMPETUOUS DUCHESS	8705	$1.25

Buy them at your local bookseller or use this handy coupon:

Bantam Books, Inc., Dept. BC, 414 East Golf Road, Des Plaines, Ill. 60016

Please send me the books I have checked above. I am enclosing $_____
(please add 35¢ to cover postage and handling). Send check or money order
—no cash or C.O.D.'s please.

Mr/Mrs/Miss_____

Address_____

City_____State/Zip_____

BC2—1/77

Please allow three weeks for delivery. This offer expires 1/78.